ACPL ITEM
DISCARDED

As we crossed the street to enter the campus, Kirsten froze and gave a little cry of surprise.

"What's wrong?" I asked.

"Do you see that girl over there?" She pointed beyond a big sign that announced to the world that it was about to enter Hartmore College. A figure slowly stepped into a pool of light from the sign. The lighting made the figure, a girl, look spooky. But even in that light, it was clear that there was something odd about her. There was a dullness, a lethargy, in the way she conducted herself.

It was as if someone was controlling her with a remote. I was only dimly aware at the time that this was my first encounter with a zombie.

★

D1010112

MYSTERY

Previously published Worldwide Mystery titles by
WENDI LEE

MISSING EDEN
DEADBEAT
HE WHO DIES

Habeas Campus

WENDI LEE

W☉RLDWIDE®

TORONTO • NEW YORK • LONDON
AMSTERDAM • PARIS • SYDNEY • HAMBURG
STOCKHOLM • ATHENS • TOKYO • MILAN
MADRID • WARSAW • BUDAPEST • AUCKLAND

If you purchased this book without a cover you should be aware
that this book is stolen property. It was reported as "unsold and
destroyed" to the publisher, and neither the author nor the
publisher has received any payment for this "stripped book."

For Beth
with much love

HABEAS CAMPUS

A Worldwide Mystery/February 2003

First published by St. Martin's Press, Incorporated.

ISBN 0-373-26447-X

Copyright © 2002 by Wendi Lee.
All rights reserved. No part of this book may be reproduced
or transmitted in any form or by any means, electronic or
mechanical, including photocopying, recording or by any
information storage and retrieval system, without permission
in writing from the publisher. For information, contact:
St. Martin's Press, Incorporated, 175 Fifth Avenue,
New York, NY 10010-7848 U.S.A.

All characters in this book are fictitious, and any resemblance to
actual persons, living or dead, is purely coincidental.

® and TM are trademarks of Harlequin Enterprises Limited.
Trademarks indicated with ® are registered in the United States
Patent and Trademark Office, the Canadian Trade Marks Office
and in other countries.

Printed in U.S.A.

Acknowledgments

I want to thank the following people: Charles Famulari for his input on the last book; Mari Famulari Katsigianis for her inspiration; Keith Kahla, Teresa Theophano, and Rich Henshaw; Dr. Hoyt Alverson; S. J. Rozan; and my husband, Terry Beatty, and my daughter, Beth, for their loving support.

ONE

IF MY FAMILY had known that I was going up to Vermont to fight zombies, they would have slapped me in an institution so fast it would have made my head spin. Hell, if *I'd* known ahead of time what I was getting myself into, I might have booked a room at the Maniac Motel myself. But this was the sort of information that my client kept to himself until I had driven the six hours and spent a luxurious night in a fabulous bed-and-breakfast. All he had told me was that it had to do with several unrelated incidents that looked suspicious. He wanted me to pose as a student and investigate possible connections. Sounded innocent enough to me.

As it turned out, my family wasn't happy with my taking off for an indefinite amount of time in the first place. And they weren't happy that I was going back to college.

"You're going *where?*" Ma had asked last Sunday as she set the plate of pasta down with a thump. Everyone at the table looked up from their dinner,

first at Ma, then at the source of Ma's agita-
tion—me.

"Vermont. For a few days. Maybe a week," I
repeated.

"Whatever for? You don't know anyone there."

"I'm going to Hartmore College."

"Whatever for?" Ma repeated.

"Maybe she's thinking of going back to school,"
Ray suggested, looking to me for help. Actually,
Ray looked pretty pleased. He'd never been crazy
about my enlisting in the Marines in the first place,
and had been less than enthusiastic when I started
my own private investigation agency. It was kind
of cool to see pride in his eyes, even if it was mis-
placed.

Vinnie laughed. "Yeah, can't you just picture it?
Angela in an Ivy League environment."

A few others around the table laughed with Vinnie—Sophia and Carla. Everyone else just stared at
me.

"What?" I asked my accusers. "I don't have a
brain? I wouldn't make it in an intellectual environment? I'm not smart enough?"

"That's not what he meant, Angie," Albert said,
glancing at Vinnie, who shrugged. A look of panic
crossed Albert's handsome face, and he looked to
his ex-wife for help. They had begun to date again
after realizing they still loved each other.

Sylvia grinned at him and leaned back in her chair. "Don't look at me. You started to say something. Go ahead and finish." She crossed her arms and turned her grin on me. A smile tugged at the corners of my mouth. I looked away before I burst out laughing. The way my family was acting about my going to Vermont, you'd think I was entering a Buddhist monastery. I briefly considered shaving my head, but decided that was too extreme.

David came to my rescue. "Put them out of their misery, Angie. Explain yourself."

I shrugged. "I've been asked to go up there to look into a small problem. Ev's close friend Don Cannon is a professor of anthropology at Hartmore College. He gave me a call yesterday. Seems he has a problem that he wants to hire me to investigate."

"What kind of problem?" Carla asked.

I had prepared an answer to satisfy the curiosity of the Matelli clan. "Um, I can't talk about my potential case right now. It's confidential."

Carla smiled. "All right. Maybe you can tell us about it when the case is finished."

Ma came up to me and patted my hand. "Sure she will. My Angela is a good girl and an ace shamus."

Lately, Ma had been on a noir binge. It started a few months ago, right after she "hired" me to find Albert, who had gone underground because people wanted him killed. Now she peppered her speech with phrases like, "You got *dat* right," and, "Take dese peas into the dining room, youse guys."

No one else seemed to have noticed her new obsession, but I'd seen the noir videos and the small pile of James M. Cain and Dashiell Hammett books from the library. She even had a Mickey Spillane book, *Vengeance Is Mine,* for bathroom reading. When Ma went on a binge, it became an obsession.

To this day, Ma believes that she helped me solve Albert's disappearance. I don't argue with her—she was a lookout for me when I broke into my brother's condo building, and she did get me in to see Don Testa, head of the Providence Mob. But she wasn't there to witness the big shootout or Albert staggering out of his captors' headquarters, a dirty rag on his hand where they'd chopped off his little finger. She didn't take Albert back to her place, burning with a fever from blood poisoning and cold from shock.

But I will never tell Ma that. And I will never bring it up to Albert. I think every Matelli is inured to Ma's little idiosyncrasies, and it's not worth pointing out this latest obsession of hers.

As I left Ma's that night, the good-byes were casual, all except Ma, who followed me outside to my car.

3 1833 04339 0522

"You gonna miss next Sunday then?" she asked me.

I shrugged. "I don't know," I said. "I'll call and let you know."

I started to leave, but she put a hand on my arm. "Because if you were sure you would be back by Sunday, I could go with you and help on this case." There was a twinkle in her eye.

"Oh, Ma," I began, but hesitated because I didn't know what to say. "Gee, that's great, but—"

She waved her hand. "Ah, of course you don't want an old lady with you."

She was a master: guilt washed over me. "Ma, it's not that I don't appreciate your help. And I may even need you to help me again. But not this time. If it were here in town, you'd be the first one I'd call...."

"You don't have to humor me, Angela Agnes. It's just a foolish old woman's dream of being useful." Her voice wavered. She was spreading it on with a butter knife.

I sighed inwardly. "Ma, we can talk about it when I get back, okay?"

Ma sighed outwardly. "Angie, ever since I helped you rescue Albert, life has been dull. I want excitement. I want to do something with my life."

I wanted to point out that raising six kids practically by herself should have been exciting enough and if I were her, I would want all the dullness I could handle, but I figured it would sound too flip.

Ma was angling to be let into my private investigation agency. It was all I could do to keep from screaming, "No! Absolutely not. I love you, but I would want to kill you, or you me, by the end of the first working day." Instead, I just swallowed my fear and smiled bravely. "This isn't a good time to talk about your career direction, Ma, but I promise when I get back—"

I don't know how Ma does it, but she gets this Keane painting look—those big-eyed children that were so popular in the 1960s and 70s. Ma can look so sad and resigned when she wants to, but this time, it wasn't working with me. I had to steel myself, but I put on my best smile, leaned over, and gave her a kiss on the cheek.

"I'll call you when I get there." I started for my Bronco.

"Sarge," Rosa called.

I stopped. "What's up, kid sister?"

"I need a key to your place if you want me to feed Fredd."

I hit my forehead. "Glad *you* remembered." I dug around in my purse until I found the extra key. Rosa normally had a key to my place, but I'd recently had the locks upgraded and hadn't gotten around to giving a key to her. I handed it over. "You got your key to the office?"

"Yup. You sure you don't want me to go along?" she asked, a grin on her pretty face. "I have more experience being a college student than you do." Rosa was the only person I'd confided in, mostly because I'd had to pick her brain about being a student.

My little sister was about to get her bachelor's degree in art history. She had originally been interested in working for a museum—possibly for the Gardner Museum—but had recently interviewed with a well-known auction house that was interested in hiring Rosa for their art department. Her specialty would be twentieth-century American and English art. Once Rosa graduated in the spring, I would have to hire someone else to work in the office and occasionally take on a surveillance job. For the moment, I didn't want to think about it. I gave Rosa a hug.

"Don't forget to bring stakes, Sarge." I looked puzzled. "To kill the zombies," she added.

I giggled. "Stakes are for vampires, you goof. I think salt is for zombies. They're supposed to be afraid of salt.'

I got in my car, which I'd packed before driving to Ma's, and drove away.

I was heading for Hartmore College, a small but

prestigious school in Bristol, Vermont. I had looked up information on the college on the Internet earlier that morning, right after my new client had called me, and it had shown me that Bristol was right on the New Hampshire border.

Nestled in the Green Mountains, Hartmore was almost an Ivy League college, but not quite. It was a little too new (established in 1891 instead of 1850 or before), but it was well-thought-of by many, and if a wealthy person couldn't get his or her son or daughter into Harvard, Princeton, or Yale, Hartmore was the next logical choice. It was said that the English department had at one time been quite good—good enough to attract the likes of Salinger and Cheever. I discovered that although their English department still held its own among the Ivy League Schools and the wanna-bes, Hartmore was becoming quite popular for those who were going into medicine and anthropology.

One of the esoteric specialties of Hartmore was a science that combined both the physical and social sciences: forensic anthropology.

Their social and physical sciences departments were considered to be as good as those of any Ivy League college due to the quality of faculty Hartmore attracted. A new medical facility had been built as an attachment to Hartmore, and it served as a teaching hospital for forensics and forensic anthropology.

My client was Dr. Don Cannon, head of the anthropology department and a very good friend of Ev Morrow, my former supervisor, current friend, and onetime client. Dr. Cannon had been hesitant to discuss the reason for his call, but he had mentioned that his field of study was Haiti, particularly voodoo, a religion that had grown to mythic proportions in America, due to the mystical rituals and monstrous tales of zombies and voodoo dolls.

"So you're telling me that you want me to come up to Vermont to hunt zombies?" I had asked, trying for the lighthearted approach.

There was a hesitation, then, "Ms. Matelli—"

"Call me Angela," I said, wondering if I'd offended Dr. Cannon.

"Angela, I would be very grateful if you would drive up here and help me sort this matter out. So far I've been left two rather clumsy anonymous warnings—a voodoo doll with pins sticking out of it and a chicken heart nailed to my door."

"No zombies yet?" I asked.

He gave a short nervous laugh. "When can you get up here? The sooner the better, as far as I'm concerned."

I thought about it, but not for long. It was clear that something was troubling Dr. Cannon, and I sensed that I hadn't gotten the entire story over the phone. At the very least, it would be a nice drive up there. What concerned me was that Dr. Cannon didn't want me to investigate openly, but undercover, as a transfer student.

He assured me that because it was only two weeks into the fall term, he could register me and would arrange for room and board as well. I would be listed as a forensic anthropology major—he promised to give me a crash course on the subject when I got there. Anyway, he told me, I wouldn't need to know more than the rudimentary elements because, according to the registration, I had just changed majors and was attending Hartmore because of their excellent medical and anthropology departments.

It was a Friday afternoon when we talked, and by the time we wrapped up the call, I had promised to drive up on Sunday night. We discussed at length how I would be presented to the college, and I reluctantly agreed to go undercover as a student. I had argued for Dr. Cannon to keep it simple—just bring me in as myself and allow me to investigate. But he was convinced that there was something dangerous going on and that to get close to the problem I needed to be there as a student rather than as an investigator.

Because of the subject matter of Cannon's problem, I immediately went out and bought a book on Haiti, voodoo, and zombies, and read it over the weekend. I came away stunned that there was such a thing as real zombies in Haiti, but as confused as ever about the religion of voodoo. Apparently the term *voodoo* was a bastardization of *vodoun,* which means the theological ideals and religious tenets of the Haitian spiritual belief system. *Vodoun* was widely practiced in Haiti, but it was more of the outer shell of the religion and only indirectly had to do with zombies. The secret societies, called the *bizango* societies, were the tribunals that stood in judgment of their members if a wrong had been committed. These societies meted out their punishments by taking a man's soul away—making that man a zombie.

I was fascinated to discover that zombies really existed. There were case histories of people who had fallen under the control of a *coup nam,* or soul spell. This was accomplished by a *coup poudre,* or powder spell, in which ingredients were ground into a powder that created a powerful poison that affected the nervous system and made the individual appear dead. After burial, the priest or sorcerer who had ordered the *coup nam* dug up the victim, who was recovering, and fed him or her a zombie paste that kept the victim under the control of the spell.

It was fascinating, but convoluted. At least I

wouldn't sound like a total idiot when talking to people who knew more than I did about the subject.

Needless to say, I saw this as a prime opportunity to mix a little pleasure with a little business. I would find the guy with the voodoo doll and the fake zombies or whatever was concerning Dr. Cannon and get a little deserved R and R as well.

BRISTOL, VERMONT, was not only near the New Hampshire border, but also only thirty miles south of Canada. The drive took me a good four hours, and I noted where all the good flea markets and antique shops were along the way so I could stop at them on my way back.

It was close to eight o'clock in the evening when I finally arrived, and I read over my directions to Dr. Cannon's house. Navigating my way around Hartmore College in the dark was interesting. I turned down a number of tiny streets that went nowhere or ended in a frat or sorority house. The mood of the campus was too quiet for my taste. I was beginning to wonder if the students were zombies. Until I happened upon a frat house.

I had parked my Bronco on a quiet street and begun to walk, looking at street signs and trying to figure out where Dr. Cannon's house was located. I hadn't found the right street to turn onto, so I walked up to a brightly lit large brick house with

Greek letters outside, hoping to find some helpful college student or, better yet, a house mother.

The door flew open, and I stepped aside to avoid being whacked. A large young man staggered out, followed by several others, all wearing T-shirts with the same Greek lettering. One of them carried a beer keg, the others carried a hose and a funnel. Some sort of rap music was pounding through the doors, and several scantily clad young women spilled out through the door, staying well back from the men who crowded around the drunk.

The first young man stumbled and finally fell to the ground. "No more," he said in a slurred voice.

A beefy blond frat boy brother laughed. "You still have two more pints to go before you break the record."

The other frat boys began chanting. It sounded like, "Go, Ray! Go, Ray!"

I heard the drunk on the grass say, "I think I'm gonna be sick." The big blond guy grabbed the drunken frat brother by the scruff of his shirt and hauled him up.

"One more, Bud." He took the keg hose and sprayed the drunken boy's face, aiming for his slack mouth.

"Excuse me," I called out. The boys fell silent and turned in unison. "I'm looking for Dr. Cannon's house."

All the boys stopped what they were doing and turned to look at me.

The blond frat boy grinned. "Well, well. Look what we have here."

I put a hand on my hip, suddenly realizing that I might be in danger from all the testosterone hovering in the air.

"What have we here?" I asked. "A stranger asking directions? A new student whom Dr. Cannon is expecting tonight?"

They hesitated. Finally the boy holding the funnel pointed it in the direction of a small street. "That's New Era Drive. Professor Cannon lives in the third house on your left."

I nodded my thanks, turned to leave, then hesitated. "Oh, I think your boy Ray is gonna hurl."

The blond frat boy looked down in time to see his victim throw up all over the front of his T-shirt and jeans.

"Shit!" Frat Boy yelled, looking down at his shirt and jeans. "Shit!"

"No, barf!" someone else piped up, and all the boys laughed in unison.

Frat Boy glared at me as if it were my fault Ray had upchucked. I shrugged, held up a hand in thanks, and left before Frat Boy got it into everyone else's heads that I might make a good gang bang.

Not that I was scared. No, not me, mistress of aikido.

Okay, if I were to be honest, I was—let's call it "cautious." I hightailed it out of sight so they would forget about little old me and concentrate on killing some poor dumb freshman with excessive alcohol.

TWO

I GOT BACK in my car and drove to Dr. Cannon's residence. Even at night, it was clearly outlined by the moonlight and the warm glow coming from inside. It was a stately English Tudor with a sloping roof, stucco siding, and a brick walkway. The dark blue Dodge Dakota sitting in the driveway was the only thing that appeared out of place in what could have been a picture postcard of a home in a small English village.

The man who opened the door looked like he would be more suited to logging work than to the ivory tower. Tall and burly, he had curly hair and a full beard, reddish brown shot with white. The only concession to the professorial image was the chrome-framed glasses. He wore casual yuppie clothes—khaki Dockers, pale yellow T-shirt, and a tan-and-gray plaid flannel overshirt. His large, well-formed feet were bare.

"Angela?"

I nodded and stuck my hand out, and we shook.

"Come in, come in," he said, stepping back to let me into the inner sanctum. He looked at his watch. "You made good time. I wasn't expecting you for another hour."

"You forget—I live in Boston."

He laughed and stepped aside. "Ah, yes. The Boston driver. So you drove straight through? You didn't stop to view the foliage?"

I shrugged. "I want foliage, I can watch my brother Vinnie fall asleep during a Celtics game." I grinned.

He laughed again. "I hope you don't mind taking off your shoes. Saves on vacuuming."

I bent down and slipped off my boots. I love the fall weather—I'm a boots-and-jeans girl, and autumn was the perfect time to wear the clothes I felt most comfortable in.

Dr. Cannon obviously hadn't hired the services of a designer—the shag carpet was burnt orange, old, and a vacuum hadn't kissed it in a long time, the brown fake velour upholstery smelled slightly damp. The only concessions to the new century were the big-screen television and accompanying DVD and CD player, and the computer in the corner on an old, ugly Salvation Army desk. The lighting was low—probably not because Dr. Cannon was some kind of ladies' man, but more likely because track lighting was too much trouble to think about installing.

I sank into one of the two easy chairs and adjusted my body so that my knees hit my chest instead of my chin. It seemed that a decorator rather than an investigator was what my potential client needed. It was hard to believe a college professor could still live like an undergraduate, but I guess being around all those young and eager kids can affect your sense of what's important and what's not. Although frankly, after my experience with the frat party, I wondered if the serious student existed only in the minds of the parents who paid for four years of keg parties.

"Can I get you something to drink?"

"No, thanks. Let's talk about your problem." I was pretty tired, and I still had to get to wherever I was going to be staying for the night.

Dr. Cannon sat down opposite me. He clasped his hands and leaned forward, resting his elbows on his knees. He started to say something, then hesitated. "I'm not sure how to begin. I'm going to sound paranoid, and you may get up at the end of my explanation and walk out."

I smiled to encourage him. "Try me. I promise I won't get up and walk away. At least not tonight." I grinned. "You're paying me to be here, remember? So tell me, why did you bring me here, and why am I going undercover as a student of forensic anthropology? I'm going to say it again— I'd rather just come up here and ask questions. Going undercover is more difficult. I have to keep up a pretense as well as ask questions."

He took off his glasses and rubbed the spot between his eyes. "I've gone over and over this in my head. I didn't have an awful lot of time to hire you, but before I did, I talked to the president of the college, who prefers to stay out of this. I only mentioned the warning I'd gotten, but I told him there were bigger ramifications here."

"The big guys never want to know what's going on," I added. "Not if it might involve legal problems."

He nodded. "Were you able to read up on the subject?"

"Just a little. Enough to know that most forensic anthropologists end up teaching at a university or working with law enforcement."

Cannon smiled. "It's a relatively new field, maybe twenty years old. Forensic anthropologists study bones and come up with physical traits."

I perked up, happy that I could discuss this subject. "Like the doctor who was called in on the case of a serial killer in California. The police and FBI had dug up a couple of acres of skulls and bones, and they needed to identify the bones of the unidentified victims. The doctor took the skulls and sculpted heads around them until they resembled the victims. From what I remember reading, the cops were able to identify a large percentage of the victims.''

Cannon was nodding. ''Yes. You need varied skills—aside from the knowledge of anthropology and biology, you need to have artistic ability as well. A lot of law enforcement agencies use forensic anthropologists in cases where they find the graves of victims of serial killers or genocide victims of dictators.''

''So how do forensic anthropology and two voodoo warnings have anything to do with my being here?''

''Less than a week ago, a student of mine, Amy Garrett, was found dead. No marks on her. She just collapsed.''

''No health problems like a weak heart or severe asthma?''

He shook his head. ''A perfect model of health. She ran every morning, was a vegetarian, and ate a low-fat diet; didn't drink, do drugs, or even stay up late.''

''You seem to have known her pretty well,'' I said, wondering if there had been more than a teacher-student relationship. It wouldn't have been the first time, and I certainly wouldn't stand in judgment of my client.

Dr. Cannon nodded, seemed to think about it, then shook his head. "It's not what you think. We weren't seeing each other. But I did consider her a friend. She was my teaching assistant's girlfriend. I'll introduce Jonathan to you tomorrow morning."

"Did she die before or after the warnings?"

"Before." He hesitated again.

"Dr. Cannon, please tell me what I'm investigating. I'm getting the impression that there's more to this tale than you're telling me."

He had the sense to look sheepish. "I saw Amy late on Thursday night, the night before I called you."

I raised my eyebrows. "How long after...?"

He hesitated again and finally said with a sigh, "The day after she died. It was from a distance of about twenty yards, but she walked under a streetlight, and I could have sworn it was her. She saw me and stretched out her hand as if she wanted help. Then she was gone."

"Sometimes light and dark can play tricks."

He shrugged. "All I can say is that it looked enough like her to give me a shock."

"Did you go after her?"

"I was in shock when I first saw her. By the time

I had the presence of mind to go after her, she'd disappeared.''

"Where did you see her?"

"Off campus on the corner of Dell and Washington.''

"Is that near a place she might have been headed for?''

"She owns—owned—a house. Jonathan had just moved in with Amy. But I didn't see her near her house. And not near the campus either.''

"The morgue?''

He thought. "It's nearer to the morgue than the campus or her house. She could have just come from there.'' He paused, stood up, and expelled a frustrated sigh. "I know how insane that sounds.''

"What time of day did you see her?''

"Night. It was about nine-thirty. I'd been out to eat—I rarely eat here—and was heading back home.''

"Did you make a report to the police?''

Dr. Cannon set his mouth in a thin line. "No. You have to understand that I have a reputation to protect.'' He shook his head. "I know that sounds like a cop-out, but—I grew up in the sixties, and if I'd heard someone saying they'd just seen a zombie, I'd think they had dropped too much acid or were having a flashback—'' He laughed.

"You don't have to apologize," I told him. "It's

admittedly weird. I was wondering if you'd made a report, because then I'd have to go through the police. As it is, I really should check in with them."

"I haven't talked to the police other than when I received the warnings."

"Then I will probably have a talk with the police about it."

He shrugged. "You're the expert."

"Did you confide in anyone at all about seeing Amy?" I asked.

"What do you mean?"

"I mean, did you find out if there's been an autopsy yet?"

He shook his head. "No. I thought I'd let you handle that."

I wasn't sure how I was supposed to do that if I was undercover as a student. "Did you talk to Amy's boyfriend? Anyone else?"

"About seeing Amy after she died? No."

If he didn't tell anyone about thinking that he saw Amy Garrett after she died, then it meant that someone saw him that night. Someone noticed that he had seen Amy. And there was a reason why no one was supposed to see her—because she was dead. Which meant that her death was more than suspicious—it might have been planned.

"You say you're positive you saw Amy, not some other girl who might have looked like her?"

"This is going to sound strange, but even though the girl looked like Amy, she didn't move like Amy."

"In what way? Are you now thinking that it's possible that the girl just looked like her?"

He made a face and shook his head. "It was Amy."

"When you said she didn't move like Amy, what did you mean?"

"Do you know what a zombie is, Angela?"

I smiled, proud that I'd boned up on the subject. "A zombie is a dead person who rises from the grave and walks among the living, at least in the movies. In real life, a zombie is someone who has ingested a poison that simulates death."

"You've been reading up on the subject." On the phone, he had suggested I read up on Haitian culture in voodoo.

I shrugged and tried to look modest. "Yes, I picked up Wade Davis's book, *Passage of Darkness: The Ethnobiology of the Haitian Zombie,* and read a bit about what real zombies are all about." I left out the fact that I'd also read Zora Neale Hurston's *Tell My Horse,* a sensational account of Haiti, voodoo and zombies.

"And the movie version of Serpent and the Rainbow isn't so far from the truth. Dr. Davis did some marvelous research that brought to light the fact that real zombies existed in Haitian culture.

"Usually, a zombie is created after a tribunal has been held and a person has been judged to have done something against the family or neighbors."

I nodded, eager to show off what I had learned. "And that person is killed, or appears to die, and rises again with the help of the *houngan,* or priest."

He nodded approval. "And that zombie becomes a slave and works for a stranger, far away from home."

We had gotten way off track—or had we? I gave him a suspicious look. "You're not suggesting that Amy Garrett is a zombie, are you?" Dr. Cannon had dragged me all the way up here to Vermont to go chasing zombies? "Look, Dr. Cannon, you probably should have hired an exorcist or one of those psychic investigators—"

He interrupted me. "Please give me a chance. This is why I didn't tell you everything over the phone. I knew you would jump to the conclusion that this is some kind of weird situation." I wanted to point out that it *was* some kind of weird situation, but I kept my thoughts to myself.

He got up and paced for a moment, then turned back to me. "If you did some reading on Haiti and voodoo and zombies, you must have suspected Amy's death was related in some way."

"Well, I—"

"From your readings, you know that zombies exist, don't you?"

I shrugged, not willing to respond, only to be cut off by his fervor and desperation.

"Angela, zombies exist, but they're not the weird horror you see on film. They're horrific, all right, but only because when you see them, you think, 'My God, I hope I didn't piss off someone enough to end up like this.' Zombification is looked upon as a social sanction. It's the equivalent of being sentenced to death, only it's the death of the soul. Your body becomes the property of the *houngan* or *bokor* who took away your soul. In Haiti, owning your soul is everything to the people. It's the one thing that can't be sold or given away. To have your soul ripped out of your body, to become a mindless creature, a shell of a human being, is worse than real death."

"I read about the *bokor*. He or she practices black magic and is often paid to make a zombie of an enemy of his or her client."

"Yes, a *bokor* uses his power for evil, to create a zombie without a tribunal. Usually for money or power or as payback for some wrong, real or imagined."

"Yeah, I read about a *bokor* who wanted a woman who was getting married to someone else.

She rebuffed his advances, then she died a few weeks later. Some time after that, someone from her village saw the woman among a group of zombies, slaves to a plantation owner or something.''

He nodded, clearly pleased with his student. ''And that's how Amy responded on the night I saw her after her death. I was in the presence of several zombies when I lived in Haiti. I know how they move, what they look like, and the Amy I saw the other night had all the symptoms.''

''And someone did this to her.'' I took a moment to formulate the turndown I was planning to hand to my soon-to-be former client. ''Look, Dr. Cannon, it's just that I'm not sure I'm the right person for this job. It's way more complicated than just someone getting his kicks sending you weird and frightening items as some sort of warning. It sounds as if whoever may have done this to Amy—if, in fact, we don't discover her body at the morgue—is warning you to forget what you saw on Thursday night.''

He looked troubled. ''Possibly. Now that you're here and we're discussing this, I realize that what I'd like you to do is prove that it *wasn't* Amy I saw, but someone else, someone who will tell me that she was there that Thursday night, right where I thought I saw Amy Garrett.''

I turned the subject back to the present problem.

"Did you attempt to call the morgue to make sure the body was still there?"

He sat back down. "See? Now that's something I definitely didn't think about. I mean, there's no one here that I can confide in who wouldn't wonder if the old professor was missing a few too many brain cells if I mentioned what I saw on Thursday night. My teaching assistant, Jonathan, would think it was some sort of sick joke, my mentioning his dead girlfriend as if she were still alive."

"So your teaching assistant doesn't know that you hired me?" I was still trying to figure out how a dead girl could be walking around campus. If Dr. Cannon had really seen her. Yeah, yeah, she got the zombie poison—but how believable was that? Why would someone do that to her? And wouldn't the medical examiner notice a dead body was missing? I was being paid to believe the impossible.

My client shook his head. "No, not yet. I haven't told anyone about you."

"So what makes you think that Amy's death wasn't just a tragedy? Have you talked to the medical examiner about checking for tetrodotoxin in her system?"

I had read up on the zombie poison. Tetrodotoxin was a neurotoxin that, when introduced to a human system, suppressed so much of the body's nervous system that it created the appearance of death. People in Haiti had often been buried under the mistaken impression that they were dead, and then would be dug up late at night in the cemetery by the person who had given them the poison. The zombie had enough physical ability to move, but he could not think for himself. Zombies were often sold to plantation owners as slave labor. They made perfect slaves for physical work.

I wondered why someone would poison Amy in such a way and, if her body wasn't in a cold storage cabinet at the medical examiner's lab, where she could be.

He shook his head. "I haven't been able to get the medical examiner to cooperate. That will be part of your job."

"You must have thought about the fact that you're receiving these warnings—do you have any idea what you're being warned about?"

He frowned and got up to pace. "I don't know. The only thing I can think of is the fact that I witnessed Amy Garrett alive."

If someone was out to get him, they would. No matter how careful he was or how many bodyguards he employed. But I didn't tell him that. I was curious about Amy Garrett, though.

"What was Amy like when she was alive?"

"Amy has always been a cheerful person—the

one who is way too perky in the morning before you have your coffee.''

I noticed that the doc used the present tense—he hadn't come to terms with the girl's death.

"But you couldn't hold it against her. She was so sweet, and very bright. She had a lot of potential.''

"If she did die under suspicious circumstances, can you elaborate? Is there something I need to know that you may not have told me?''

"In the last few days before she died, she was distracted, troubled. She came up to me at one point and asked if she could talk to me but she wouldn't tell me what was bothering her. We scheduled a time in the late afternoon. But later that day, she called to tell me she didn't feel well and would have to reschedule. She died the next day. Jonathan found her that night, dead in the house they shared.''

"What was her major?'' I was pretty sure I knew the answer already.

"Forensic anthropology.'' Which was why he'd given me the cover of being a student of forensic anthropology.

"You still haven't told me why you suspect that she was murdered.'' It was getting late, and I was tired. I still wasn't sure where I was staying for the night.

Cannon nodded, seeming to understand my weariness as well as my desire to get to the point.

"The fact that she seemed distracted, the fact that she appeared to change overnight. I don't know. I just have a feeling she had something she wanted to tell me, then she died. It was strange." I had a feeling Cannon had something he wanted to tell me, but was holding back.

"Let's get to the warnings."

"The morning after I saw Amy walking around the campus, I received the voodoo doll." Cannon got up and paced, one hand in his pocket. I could imagine him lecturing—this was probably his style, very relaxed and interested in his subject, and he was able to transfer that enthusiasm to a classroom full of students. I might have stayed in college if I'd had more teachers like him.

"A student could have left it there as a joke."

He nodded. "I thought of that. Although I'm afraid I thought it was someone who didn't like my classes, or who had gotten a worse grade than he'd expected, because there were pins stuck in the heart and the head."

"So that didn't bother you much?"

He shook his head. "No. I brushed it off and kept the voodoo doll in a box in my office file cabinet. But yesterday morning, I stopped by the office to clear up some paperwork, and found a chicken heart stuck to my office door with a long nail.''

"Not such a joke."

He looked grim. "I'm just glad I went in today— the smell after the weekend would have been hard to cover up."

"I take it you didn't store the chicken heart away in a file drawer."

"I called in the campus police. It was Saturday, so they contacted the office staff and other professors at their homes, and I guess they're going to question some of the students I've had some trouble with."

I held up my hand. "Don't tell me—they're looking at it as some tasteless practical joke."

His bleak smile was affirmative. "So that's where we stand."

I had two bad practical jokes and a student who might or might not have been killed.

THREE

AFTER WE SIGNED the agreement and he gave me a retainer check, Dr. Cannon put me up in a nearby bed-and-breakfast for the night. If I'd gotten to town earlier, I might have had a little time to enjoy the room and private bath. As it was, I was in bed by midnight and up by seven in the morning. The breakfast was fabulous—strong French roast coffee, fresh-squeezed orange juice, cranberry muffins with pecan streusel topping, a fluffy asparagus and baby Swiss omelet, and Virginia ham. I sat in the dining area, where the owners had installed a large picture window that looked out on a forest of foliage turning russet, gold, bronze, and orange. The setting was tranquil, perfect. I never wanted to leave.

Dr. Cannon had gone to a lot of expense. He could have just stuck me in a cheap roach motel with nearby ice and pop machines, but he went to a lot of trouble to put me up in a place that made me want to stay in bed until noon. I had a feeling this would be the last peaceful moment I would have until this case ended.

I packed my bags and said good-bye to the big fluffy bed and private bath, the savory breakfast, and the spectacular setting, then headed out to the Hartmore campus. Dr. Cannon had given me a map of the campus, and marked off the places where I needed to go. He had already registered me as a student, and had instructed me to pick up my schedule at the registration office.

The office was located on the second floor of the Student Union. I walked in the door marked "Student Services." It was a large room with half a dozen desks scattered behind a large counter that separated most of the room from the students. There were already quite a few students crammed into the small waiting area, and I took my place in line. After more than half an hour of waiting, I was finally at the front of the line. I gave my name to the woman, a matronly sort with a pair of out-of-date plastic glasses, and she came back with a packet that explained my class schedule and my dormitory room assignment.

I was treated with some deference because Dr. Cannon had personally seen to my registration. Cannon told me that he had sent in my registration on Friday after talking to the dean of students about shuttling me through the system quickly. He'd explained that I was the daughter of a close friend of his. It had worked, and my cover now was that I was an anthropology major who had transferred from a college overseas, in Poland. He had explained to the dean that my transcripts would take a few weeks, possibly a month, to be sent over here. The dean accepted this, mostly because Dr. Cannon was well regarded at the college.

Before taking on this case, I had checked up on my client. Even though Ev Morrow had recommended me to Cannon, I thought it would be sensible to do a little digging into his background to make sure there wasn't a rape charge or some other surprise in store for me. I had asked my cousin, Antonia, to come up with a quick background on him. Antonia was the Cindy Crawford of computers. It was hard to believe that she wasn't a supermodel instead of a nerdy computer hacker. She had her own consulting business, and with only a few exceptions—myself included—worked exclusively for very wealthy people with computer problems. Rumor had it that she had worked for Bill Gates himself, but she had never confirmed it.

According to the background check, Donald Michael Cannon had grown up in the Midwest—Edina, Minnesota, to be exact. He had attended the University of Minnesota and graduated with a major in anthropology. He had gone on to get a master's in biology at the University of Wisconsin at Madison in 1976. He worked for one of the foremost authorities in the ethnobiology field, and they spent the next two years in the Caribbean, island-hopping and collecting samples of indigenous plants to study for medicinal purposes.

When the study was over, Cannon returned to the States and got his Ph.D. in teaching. He promptly applied for and was given a grant to study voodoo in Haiti for another two years. He came back home with several research papers under his belt linking certain medicinal drugs to religious practices—voodoo specifically. After writing several articles on the practice of voodoo and the zombie phenomenon, Cannon began teaching at Hartmore. He had been at the college since 1983, publishing numerous papers on the properties of tetrodotoxin and its effects on Haitian society, specifically voodoo and zombies as a social sanction. He had tenure, had gone through a marriage, a divorce, and a second marriage that didn't take, and had finally settled into bachelorhood in the late 1990s. He had one grown son who was a lawyer and a daughter who was attending Harvard, majoring in business and computers. No Indiana Jones, Jr., either of his kids.

He'd had one DUI ticket back in 1991, the year his first marriage failed. There was nothing that indicated why his marriage failed—no domestic violence charges, nothing like that. The second marriage came almost immediately after the divorce, and I gathered that maybe there'd been an affair. The second marriage lasted barely a year.

I stopped looking after that. It seemed that Cannon's background was clear of prison terms and other legal problems. Whether he'd cheated on his first wife and been caught, resulting in a divorce— that was none of my business. I figure that when I start projecting situations onto facts, if I'm not being paid to do a background check, I should stop. I'd done my job. He was clean. I was fairly sure I wasn't being brought in to clean up someone else's dirty laundry.

I kept my car parked where it was and walked to the social sciences building, which was all the way across campus. The administrative buildings, the chapel, and the Student Center seemed to be grouped at one end of the campus, the dorms, sororities and fraternities next, and the teaching departments and classrooms at the far end, away from the administrative part.

The social sciences building was called the Oscar P. Wilson Building, and was named after, no doubt, some rich guy who gave the college money, which hadn't been used on a new building—this was an old red brick building with white trim and cornices.

It was ivy-covered red brick, almost a cliche, but I immediately liked it.

Inside, several students were milling around, holding cups of Starbucks coffee, bleary-eyed, trying to wake up. One girl was curled up in the corner of the stairwell, a book open, taking notes.

I went up to her. She seemed as if she might be able to help me. "Excuse me. I'm looking for the anthropology department."

"Third floor." She didn't look up or smile, just kept scribbling something in her notebook, flipped the page of her book, ignored me.

Realizing that she had given me the information, I stifled the urge to give her the finger and moved on with a muttered "thank you." I tried to remember that it was barely eight o'clock and most of these kids had probably been up late last night studying. I thought back to the frat boys I'd encountered and amended that to partying.

The third floor was filled with tiny hallways that I had a hard time imagining Dr. Cannon getting through. His broad shoulders probably brushed the walls on either side as he walked down to his office, which was at the end.

He was in the office, and looked as if he'd been in for a few hours. The office was small, but it had a window. Books were stacked up in piles on the floor if they weren't shelved in bookcases that lined the walls. His desk took up half the room, and there were two chairs, one for the desk and one for students who were meeting with him.

His desk had a notebook computer and small desktop printer, and stacks and stacks of papers on every surface inch. The unoccupied chair had papers on it, and I hesitated to move them. My client belatedly noticed the papers and rushed to clear them, sending them in an avalanche onto the floor.

"Love the decor," I said, sitting down gingerly.

He grinned. "My maid is on vacation. Permanently." He got up, squeezed past me to the filing cabinet, which seemed to be swallowed up by the minutiae that filled the space. With some difficulty, he opened a drawer, pulled out a shoebox, and handed it to me. "This is the little present that was left on my desk."

I opened it carefully and inspected the contents. The doll was crudely hand sewn, looking somewhat like Dr. Cannon—the perp had made a small pair of wire-rimmed glasses, probably the thing that took the most time, other than picking the lock of the office to leave this memento on the professor's desk.

I checked with Dr. Cannon. "You lock your office every night?"

"Of course. I don't have a Ph.D. for nothing."

"Who else has a key?"

"Jonathan Sharpe, my assistant." He frowned, thinking. "I'm pretty sure he'd given his girlfriend a copy. Amy sometimes left papers on my desk if she was heading back to the campus library to study. If she had a test to study for, or if she got up early to go to the lab to meet Dr. Rathman, she would stop by my office and drop off the papers."

I looked back in the box. There were two Polaroids of the chicken heart that had been nailed to the door. I studied them, but there wasn't anything that jumped out at me other than the fact that some sicko had taken a chicken organ and nailed it to a door. Yuck.

"That's a voodoo warning?" I asked.

Dr. Cannon smiled. It wasn't a patronizing smile, but it promised that I didn't know much about voodoo. I held up my hands. "Hey, all I know about voodoo is what I see on TV and the little I've read of Wade Davis's book."

He reached behind him and came back with a thin book, handing it to me. "Might as well do a little more research while you're here."

"Ooh, homework already?" I took the book: *Voodoo Practices in Haiti.*

"There'll be a test at the end of the week," he said with a grin, then turned serious. "To answer your question, I suppose it was a clumsy attempt at a warning." He had hunched his shoulders, resting his elbows on the arms of his chair, and clasped his hands in front of his body. "I'm not saying that a *bokor,* a black magic sorcerer to you, wouldn't send a warning to someone they considered a threat, but they wouldn't use a heart from a supermarket chicken."

I blinked. "Did I hear you right?"

He nodded. "Yep, that much the police were able to tell. It was a heart from a packaged chicken. There were even some giblets clinging to it."

I didn't know exactly what giblets were, just that I only ate them if they were in a gravy or dressing for a turkey.

"Can you think of anyone who might have a grudge against you?"

He laughed. "Probably hundreds of students over the years, a few faculty members."

"Can you make me a list?"

"Sure. I'll get that to you by the end of the day."

"Let's talk about Jonathan. Did you mention these warnings to him?"

"He was with me when I discovered the doll."

"He was working after his girlfriend died?" Most grief-stricken people would take a day off. But it wasn't a hard-and-fast rule.

"He told me that he'd rather be working than sitting around in an empty house with reminders of her surrounding him. When he saw the doll, he thought it was a joke. Kirsten teased me about it.''

"Kirsten?" This was a new name for me to take in.

"Kirsten Sorenson-Andersen. She's working on her doctorate here at Hartmore."

"Doctorate in what?"

"Ethnobotany. She's on a grant as a lecturer, and teaching a course this term."

I waved my hands in the air. "Okay, okay. I've heard of ethnobiology, but not ethnobotany. What's the difference?"

"Ethnobiology is the study of man and how the indigenous flora and fauna relate to his needs. Ethnobotany is a branch of ethnobiology that focuses strictly on man's relationship to the plants around him. My specialty is Haiti and voodoo culture, how plants and animals are used in a cultural and spiritual belief system."

"Okay, I understand now, I think."

He looked at his watch. "I have a nine o'clock class. Did you want to come with me?"

I supposed my dorm room would wait. I consulted my class schedule. "I guess I have to go with you. I'm supposed to be in that class."

"That class" was Introduction to Anthropology 101. Basic stuff. Dr. Cannon had thought of everything—he had books for all my courses. "You wouldn't believe the stories I had to tell the other instructors to get them to part with a copy of the courses I signed you up for,'' he told me as we walked out of the office. ''Jonathan should be at this class. I can introduce you.''

The class was in a small square white box of a room on the second floor. A large chalkboard took up one wall, with an easel propped on the side for other visual aids. Dr. Cannon had given me a pile of handouts that were titled ''Art and Religion in Haiti.''

There were long tables around the room, and several students were already sitting at them, some studying a chapter, some talking quietly and taking notes. None of them took the slightest notice of me, which made me more uncomfortable than if they'd looked at me with open curiosity. From my own experience with higher education about ten years ago, I recalled that this was an attitude that all college students assumed like a mantle, whatever that was.

My client, now my professor, asked me to hand out the papers, which I did. After he checked his material over once more, a few more students straggled in just under the deadline, Dr. Cannon began his lecture. ''Today we're going to focus on art and how it integrates into society and specifically into the Haitian belief system...''

I sat halfway down a table against the far wall. Fifteen minutes into his lecture, another student slipped into the room. He was of average height, thin, with good cheekbones, and he had dark good looks that included a cleft in his chin and two slashes for eyebrows. He wore chinos and a blue shirt with the sleeves rolled up. There was a five o'clock shadow on his jawline that seemed to be more carefully crafted than legitimately earned. Cannon nodded briefly to him, and the student laconically nodded back. I noted that he carried no book bag, not even a notebook and pen.

"As I was saying," Cannon continued, "we look at a snake and recoil in horror. The average Haitian, someone who has had contact with voodoo beliefs, sees the snake, or the serpent, as a symbol of change, life and death, and a symbol of wisdom. Their god is Damballah Wedo, the Great Serpent, who is the Father of Creation."

I listened in fascination as Cannon wove the symbolism of Haitian art into voodoo beliefs. I wanted to have a notebook. It had been so long since I'd been in college—but if I'd had more instructors like Dr. Cannon, I might have stayed there for the entire four years. Then I might not have entered the Marines, and I wouldn't have been where I was today. Here.

Dr. Cannon wound up his lecture, leaving time for students to ask questions. He answered patiently. Jonathan, or the student I assumed was Jonathan, still sat with his head inclined, his hands clasped in front of him on the table.

"On Wednesday, I expect to see your papers turned in. No more than ten pages on some aspect of the voodoo religion," Dr. Cannon announced above the rustle of papers, the unzipping of book bags, and the scraping of chairs on the linoleum floor. "If you're having problems with your subject, today is the last day you can talk to me or to Jonathan about it."

Several earnest-looking students clustered around Dr. Cannon with questions while a couple of attractive female students made a beeline for the good-looking grad student.

I waited until Cannon had patiently answered all the students' questions, and then he called Jonathan over. The students who had been monopolizing his time reluctantly left, one tall, slender girl slipping a piece of paper to him, no doubt with her name and phone number on it. She probably figured, hey, Amy isn't around anymore, here's one perfectly good, slightly used man, might as well get my bid in now.

The girl had long blond hair that had clearly been to a salon for that spiral perm. She wore a long formfitting black dress that was more appropriate for a cocktail party than for a classroom, but she didn't seem to notice.

"Jonathan, this is Angela Matelli. She just transferred here from abroad."

Jonathan smiled, although I noticed that his eyes were sad. "Nice to meet you. Where did you go to school?"

I looked to Dr. Cannon for help. We hadn't really discussed that.

"Er, the university in Poland," he said.

"That's right," I replied.

Jonathan frowned. "I didn't know they had an anthropology department."

"That's why I transferred back to the States."

"What made you choose Hartmore?" Jonathan asked. We were all walking out of the room by now, heading back to Dr. Cannon's office.

"Umm, well, I...have an uncle who went here, a great-uncle, and I thought I'd try my luck here. Actually, I didn't really think of majoring in anthropology until last summer"—I was getting into my story—"when I was on a dig in Ireland. Just for a lark."

Jonathan looked at me as if I'd lost my mind. I'd remembered reading something about a dig in Ireland recently and felt on fairly safe territory, unless he asked me more-specific questions. I was counting on Cannon to save my bacon.

"That Viking excavation, you know," Professor Cannon added, coming to my rescue.

"Did you find anything interesting?" Jonathan asked.

My client changed the subject abruptly. "Here we are," Cannon said, maybe a little too heartily. "Angela needs to get settled in her dorm room. Maybe we can continue this conversation tonight. I thought, a pizza party to welcome Angela?"

Jonathan was quiet for a moment, then nodded. "Sure, that sounds fine."

Cannon turned to me and, for the sake of Jonathan, explained about Amy.

I put on my concerned face, which wasn't hard to do. Jonathan clearly was suffering, which was probably what made him attractive to the girl who had slipped her number to him.

"I am so sorry to hear that. She sounds like she was very intelligent."

Jonathan perked up a bit. "Do you have lunch plans?"

I shook my head. "I just arrived this morning in time for Dr. Cannon's class. I haven't even had time to check out my dorm room."

He suddenly seemed friendlier to me, less remote. "Would you like a tour of the campus after you're settled? I have a couple of free hours for lunch. My treat."

"I'd like that. Thank you." I gave him my dorm and room number, and I said good-bye to Cannon and Jonathan and left to find my dorm room.

FOUR

As I HOOFED IT across campus back toward the dormitories, I noticed that a lot of girls here wore either jeans or long dresses, or skirts with twin sets. I would be in the former category, wearing jeans and T-shirts. I might pick up a flannel overshirt to fit in. Most students carried a book bag, so I made a note to pick one up.

My room was in a dormitory called Chapin Hall. I pulled my Bronco into a space behind the building and took my suitcase and another bag out, the one with my notebook computer. Chapin Hall had been built in the 1970s—low, yellow brick with plain utility windows and glass doors. It was depressing. Inside, if you didn't know any better, you might think it was a really bad nursing home, except there was no smell of disinfectant. The linoleum tiles were beige with dark red streaks, the walls were Sheetrock painted white, with cheap pine baseboards stained to look like oak. The doors to the rooms were hollow. It amazed me to think that students actually lived here for four years and didn't think about killing themselves.

I passed one room that was open—no door to it—and saw a television set and lots of broken-in furniture—two sofas, four easy chairs, a dozen big pillows. There was a carpet pulled up from the floor that had been rolled up and taken out to the hallway. A large paper-wrapped carpet was in the room, ready to be installed.

I had expected to get a room by myself, but Dr. Cannon had explained, apologetically, that there was only one bed open in the dorms, and it was in a double room. I opened the door to room 133 with my key and encountered chaos. Clothes were thrown on the floor in a pile, both beds looked as if someone had slept in them, the closet door stood open, and clothes half on, half off hangers, more clothes on the floor of the closet. Both beds were rumpled, unmade, a small microwave sat on a nightstand by one bed, the door standing open, the lightbulb burning. A plate of crusted pizza remains sat on top of the microwave, and a bowl of potato chips sat on the floor near the bed, with some chips artfully scattered around the bowl.

I tiptoed through the mess, determined which bed was most likely my roomie's, and took the other one. I stripped the bed, put on it the fresh sheets

that I'd brought with me, and put my suitcase on
top of the freshly made bed.

Both desks were being used, but one desk had
papers and books piled on top of it, and these were
easy enough to move. I took piles of the papers and
books and stacked them next to my roomie's bed,
with a note apologizing for moving some of her
things. I set up my notebook computer and small
printer on the desk. I had to make it look like I was
a student. Eventually, Dr. Cannon and I would have
to take some people into our confidence—we would
be visiting the police about Amy's autopsy in the
next day or two.

Next, I put my clothes away in the closest
dresser. Fortunately, the dresser nearest my new
bed hadn't been used—probably because my roommate had always preferred to put her clothes on the
floor.

There was a knock at my door. I opened it to
find a young girl wearing an orange pullover sweat-
shirt and a long black, orange, and green skirt. Her
reddish hair was up in high pigtails with butterfly
clips, and she wore glitter on her face. I always
thought that glitter makeup was okay at night if you
were going out clubbing, but it looked weird when
a girl wore it in the day.

''Oh.'' She looked disappointed when she saw
me, then checked the room number one more time.

"Um, is Savanna here?" So that was my room-mate's name. The girl studied me as if trying to figure out why I was in Savanna's room.

"Can I take a message?"

The girl before me winced. "Savanna hasn't met you yet, has she?"

"What?" I asked, wondering if she was wincing for me or for Savanna.

She shook her head. "I just don't think the two of you are going to get along. You're absolutely the opposite of Savanna."

I leaned on the door frame and crossed my arms. "A lot of times opposites attract."

She didn't look convinced. "Savanna is—kind of particular."

Another voice joined us from down the hall. "Roxie! Ready for lunch?" Her voice died down when she encountered me in the door of the room. Savanna was the blond girl from my anthropology class, the one who looked as if she viewed every woman as competition. Probably the reason Roxie was a friend was that she was of some use to Savanna. Of course, this was all just my opinion. Savanna could turn out to be a wonderful, sweet girl who had numerous female friends and believed in feminism.

"What are you doing in my room?" She was

frowning, pouting almost. Oops, guess I was right. She hated competition.

"Hi, I'm your new roommate. Angela Matelli." I stuck out my hand. She recoiled and looked at my palm as if I'd presented her with a bug.

"But it's halfway through the term. How could anyone transfer here this late?"

I shrugged. "I dunno, but I did. And it's not quite midterm yet. Just a couple of weeks, really." I crossed my arms for lack of anything better to do. Then I stepped back and said, "Look, you weren't here so I went ahead and took one of the beds—" Before I could finish my sentence, which included an apology for my presumption, she brushed past me and stood in the center of the room.

"What have you done!?" she screeched.

I looked over at Roxie, who raised her eyebrows and shrugged her shoulders. Oh, boy, now I had a prima donna for a roommate. I went into the room.

"What do you mean, what have I done? I think I was pretty agreeable, considering that I'm rooming with a guy."

Savanna spun around and got in my face. "Do *I* look like a guy?"

I tried to remain cool. What I really wanted to do was perform the aikido submission hold *ikiyo* on her wrist until she cried uncle. "No, but you sure live like one. What kind of a mess do you call this?"

"*My* mess. And you had no right to touch it." She put her hands on her slender hips, and I had an urge to force-feed Ding-Dongs to her. Then I remembered the bowl of potato chips and plate of pizza remains and realized that it probably wouldn't work.

"I only touched what was on *my* side of the room." I sounded as petulant as Savanna did. I was starting to wonder if I could get a room change before I started crying and asking for my Barbie doll back when another voice interrupted us.

"Am I interrupting something?" Jonathan stood in the doorway, Roxie right behind him, watching the action unfold and wearing an amused look. Jonathan looked uncertainly at both of us. I immediately felt embarrassed for Savanna and the way she was behaving, but apparently I was the only one who did.

She put on a dazzling smile and slithered over to him. "Jonathan! I wasn't expecting you." She started to take his arm, but he shifted away from her, almost as if this was a practiced move.

"I didn't realize you two would be rooming together."

I crossed my arms, tried to smile, and shot a mild look at Savanna. "Neither did I."

Jonathan transferred his attention from Savanna to me. "You ready for lunch and a campus tour?"

I smiled. "I think so." I looked over at Savanna. "I hope we can talk about this later."

She didn't say anything, just shot a narrow look at me. I started to worry about my notebook computer. Would she pour coffee on it? And what about my clothes—would I come back to find them shredded?

"Shall we go?" Jonathan asked.

I looked over and nodded. I smiled at her as I went out the door.

JONATHAN TOOK ME to the Wild Onion Cafeteria in the Student Union. It was unlike the student cafeteria I used to go to when I was taking classes. Ten years ago at the University of Massachusetts, my choices were hamburgers, pizza, and grilled cheese sandwiches. This Wild Onion Cafeteria was like a fine delibakery. Exotic, healthful choices were side by side with the cholesterol specials.

I ordered a roasted vegetable sandwich—eggplant, red pepper, zucchini, yellow squash, and red onion with goat cheese and pesto sauce on sesame semolina bread. Jonathan had a tuna melt.

"I could get used to this," I said as we sat by one of the windows overlooking the campus center, which was a big open grassy area where students could sun themselves, play Frisbee, folkdance, or just enjoy a few minutes of the outdoors before the English lit midterm.

Jonathan laughed. "You sound as if you won't be here for very long. What year are you?"

I hadn't really thought much about my cover story. At least, not details like this. I looked young for my almost thirty years. "I'm in my third year."

Jonathan cocked his head. "Really? Please don't get me wrong, but you seem mature enough to be working on your master's."

So much for looking young. He seemed to realize his gaffe and quickly said, "Not that you don't look like you belong here, but your attitude seems, well, more confident than the attitude of a lot of these students."

After the little scene with Savanna where we almost got into a hair-pulling contest, I was surprised he thought that. I decided a little truth wouldn't hurt. "I spent some time in the Marines before deciding to go back to college."

He nodded. "Sounds interesting. What's your major?"

"Forensic anthropology."

His expression turned to stone. Hard for me to miss that switch.

"Did I say something wrong?"

"No, no," he said, shaking his head. "My girl-friend, Amy, was a forensic anthropology major."

"I'm sorry. If you don't mind my asking, I understand that she just collapsed?"

He looked as if he were going to cry, then got himself under control. "Actually, she hadn't been feeling well that day. She was sleeping in our bed when I found her."

"Did she have some kind of flu?"

He paused as if to think about it. "Maybe. She was pale, sluggish. She'd vomited that morning before she died. She told me she felt as though her skin was on fire. I wanted to take her to the hospital to be looked at, but she said she thought she'd be all right if she just got enough sleep. She'd been pushing herself pretty hard to get her thesis finished."

"Did she have any health problems?" I'd asked Dr. Cannon, but Jonathan had to know more than my client did. After all, he had lived with her.

"No. No, she didn't. Amy was one of the healthiest people I knew. She was a rock climber, she was into parasailing, running six miles every morning, she was a vegetarian, and she didn't drink or do drugs."

I'd heard that before, but he clearly needed to talk about her.

"Have they figured out what caused her death?"

He shook his head. "It's been about a week, and we haven't heard anything from the medical examiner."

That wasn't unusual. Forensic pathologists tend to be county employees and, in a state like Vermont, usually have a large area to cover. "What about her family?"

"Her parents died when she was seven. She was an only child. Her grandmother raised her, but she passed away last year. Amy was very close to her grandmother and was very sad that her grandma didn't live to see her get her doctorate."

"So who has any say over what happens to the body?" My bluntly put question made me cringe, but Jonathan was so miserable that he didn't seem to notice.

"The county, of course. Mysterious death. But because there wasn't a will, her estate—"

"Estate?"

"Amy's parents and grandmother left her very well-off. But her estate is being handled by the government now."

I nodded, my mind working. Hmmm. A motive, if her mysterious collapse involved poison. But who collected? There was no will; she died intestate. No one profited except the state. I thought about looking into insurance, but again, that seemed far-fetched.

Amy was wealthy, so why would someone kill her to collect on insurance? All that money lying there, going to waste. I thought about starting a background check—and maybe some obscure relative or an insurance policy held by Jonathan would come out of the woodwork. I made a mental note to ask Dr. Cannon about local computer geeks who could be discreet.

I changed subjects. "Dr. Cannon told me about a couple of strange things that were left for him."

Jonathan brightened a little. "Yes, voodoo warnings." He chuckled. "Or someone's idea of what voodoo is all about."

"You mean voodoo dolls aren't used?"

He shrugged. "More in the movies than anywhere else. How familiar are you with Haiti and voodoo?"

I grinned. "I saw *Serpent and the Rainbow*. I read a book on Haiti and zombies. That's why I'm taking classes in anthropology now. I decided that I would be interested in learning more about the cultural end of ethnobiology. Maybe I'll change my major again. I don't know. But I'm really a babe in the woods." I knew that I couldn't keep up with the knowledge of Haiti that Jonathan possessed, so I wasn't even going to pretend. I was glad that Dr. Cannon had kept my background simple.

"Well, what Dr. Cannon received is called a

wanga, a malevolent magical charm. It's a warning.''

''A warning for what?'' I asked.

Jonathan smiled, but there was no warmth there. ''Only Dr. Cannon can tell us that. And he isn't sure what he's being warned about.''

After we finished our lunch, Jonathan took me on a tour of the campus, skipping the administrative buildings but including the campus movie theater, the stage where both music concerts and plays were put on, and the campus bookstore.

''Do you need any of your books for courses?'' he asked.

''Oh, no,'' I replied without thinking, ''Dr. Cannon bought my books for me.''

Jonathan gave me a strange look.

''I mean,'' I amended, ''I requested that he buy them and I'd pay him back. He knew that I'd be coming here from abroad, and he wanted to help me out with getting adjusted to Hartmore as quickly as possible.''

''Where were you living in Poland?''

''On campus. In Krakow.'' God, I hoped I was right—I knew Krakow was in Poland. I didn't know if the University was located there. I didn't know why we hadn't just said I was going back to school. It would have made more sense, but my client had explained that I would fit in better if I'd been in college a few years and was finally settling down to a major here at Hartmore. Students transferred all the time to get into a specialty field. It made sense.

"So you had some background in medicine already, right? You were planning on being a doctor?"

American students who couldn't get into medical school sometimes went overseas to get their medical degrees. Poland had a good medical program. I would never be a doctor, but at least I could pretend to be premed. I shrugged in answer to his question.

"My folks wanted me to be a doctor," I said. Which was half the truth—Ma wanted me to *marry* a doctor, but had never expressed an interest in what I did for a living until recently. "But I don't have a great bedside manner. I'm not interested in going into research, but I do have an artistic side, especially for something hands-on like sculpting. Forensic anthropology seemed to fit the bill." I didn't mention that all my sculptures would look the same—lumpy, two holes poked in for eyes, a slash for the mouth, and a smaller lump for a nose.

"You would have enjoyed getting to know Amy. She would have loved to show you around the lab where she worked."

"She worked at a forensics lab?"

He nodded. "She was good at sculpture, but a wiz at reconstructing faces on computer graphics."

"You sound very proud of her."

He had a faraway gleam in his eye. "We were going to be married as soon as we got our doctorates. She was closer than I was. I think she could have graduated in December, but Amy was willing to wait for me to finish my degree in May. She turned down a job offer in Houston to stay here another six months."

"I'm sorry I never got a chance to meet her." And I was. "Dr. Cannon told me he thought she was too healthy to have collapsed like that."

Jonathan looked at me strangely. "He's right about that. But I guess the medical examiner is waiting for the state forensic pathologist to visit. We won't know what caused her death for a few more days." He looked at his watch. "Oh, sorry. I have to go. An appointment with my thesis."

"Thanks for showing me around and making me feel welcome."

He stood up, and I followed him out of the Wild Onion. "You're coming to the pizza party tonight?"

I shrugged. "I guess so. It's in my honor."

He laughed. "Yeah, Dr. Cannon makes us all feel special."

I touched his arm. "Then why would someone want to send him those warnings?"

He paused and nodded. "He and I discussed it at length, and he swears he has no idea why someone is sending him those weird warnings. We went through every possibility we could think of, and nothing seemed to push a button with him."

I shook my head. "He has no enemies, but maybe there's some student who might have received a lower grade than he or she expected."

Jonathan ran a hand over the back of his neck, a sign to me that our conversation bothered him more than he let on.

"Look, you'd better keep that date with your thesis," I said. "We can talk about this later tonight. I have something I need to do as well."

We parted amicably, and I headed for my Bronco. I decided it was time to introduce myself to the police. It was time to call Lee Randolph, my poker buddy and according to Ma my best chance to get married now that Reg had escaped my desperate grasp. Lee and I had hit it off the moment we met over my first case. He didn't have any of the attitude about private investigators that a lot of cops have. Of course, it helped that we were both Marines. He'd served earlier than I had, during Vietnam. I lucked out and served in peacetime, post-Gulf War.

After I'd gotten off the phone with Dr. Cannon on Friday, I called Lee and asked if he could pave the way for me in Bristol. It happened that one of his state patrol buddies was from the area, and had grown up with one of the sergeants on the force in Bristol.

I drove to the station, which was located only a few blocks from the college. The station was in a small redbrick building, probably built in the late 1700s or early 1800s. As I looked around Bristol, I noticed that it was an upscale small town—several antique shops, boutiques, and trendy little eateries lined the main street, which was called, strangely enough, Main Street. Bristol was also home to Bristol Outdoors, a trendy L. L. Bean sort of place. There was a factory and an outlet, and it was always in fashion to stop in Bristol for a pair of hiking boots or jeans or for camping equipment.

Inside the station, there was an open room with several police officers at their desks. Most of them tried to look busy—it didn't appear to bother them if they just sat there and whittled or did whatever idle law enforcement officers did these days. Let's just say that no one jumped up and fell all over himself to help me. And I guess there wasn't enough crime in Bristol for them to have a security door installed. Apparently I could have entered with an Uzi and wiped out the entire police force in less than thirty seconds, if I'd wanted to.

I walked up to the nearest officer, a thirtyish, stocky, balding man who looked very uncomfortable in his uniform. Either the uniform had shrunk, or the officer had gained some weight, because he kept shifting positions and running a finger between his collar and neck as if that act would stretch the already tight circumference.

"Excuse me, Officer, could you tell me where I could find Sergeant Peter Zymm?"

"Ayeah." The officer turned and said in a slightly louder voice, "Peter, you have a visitor." Only he didn't pronounce his *r*'s, and it came out, "Petah, you have a visitah."

A man came over. He was in his early forties, and had incredibly nice wavy golden hair and a face pitted with acne scars. But he had the nicest eyes I'd ever seen. Warm golden eyes and a killer smile. "May I help you?"

I stuck out my hand and introduced myself. "Jason Hughes may have contacted you already, I hope."

He shook my hand. His grip was firm. "Ayeah, Jason. How is he doing down in Massachusetts?"

"Sergeant Zymm, to be honest with you, I don't know him. I know Lee Randolph of the BPD, and he knows Jason."

Zymm took it all in and seemed to consider it. "Ayeah, I've heard of Lieutenant Randolph from Jason. Used ta play poker tagether when they were stationed in the Marines."

"I met Lieutenant Randolph during a case, and we have the same military background."

"You were a Marine?" Interest sparked in Zymm's eyes.

I nodded. "Criminal Investigations the last few years. I also play a mean game of poker."

Zymm gestured to a desk and two chairs. We sat. "Maybe you can sit in on a game."

"If I'm here long enough." The prospect was daunting. I turned his attention to the subject at hand. "You're familiar with Dr. Donald Cannon?"

"Ayeah, professor of anthropology. He's had some trouble at the college. A voodoo doll comes to mind."

I nodded and filled him in on why I was here. I didn't tell him that my client claimed to have seen Amy Garrett up and about, but I did have to tell him a partial truth.

"There was a sighting the other night. Someone, I can't say who, saw Amy Garrett wandering around Bristol late on Thursday night."

"Can you tell me who?"

"Sorry, that's confidential." I felt like an idiot

even mentioning this, but I wanted to see what Zymm's reaction would be.

"So you're telling me that Dr. Cannon has hired you to find out if Ms. Garrett is a zombie?"

I shrugged. "Zombies exist in Haiti. Why not here?" I could see I was losing him. Zymm gave me a look that told me he thought I was a crackpot. I explained about the zombie poison. He stopped looking at me askance, but was clearly reserving judgment. It was too foreign an idea to absorb quickly.

"Well, Ms. Matelli, I admit it is a possibility, but it's still a bit of a stretch. My first question would be, why would anyone feed this zombie poison to Ms. Garrett to fake her death?"

I nodded. "I wish I could give you an answer, but I'm not even sure that Amy Garrett's body is missing from the morgue. I can't go very far in that direction until I know if it's even possible that she hasn't really died." I leaned forward. "Actually, this may all be resolved if I find out that her body is still at the morgue."

"That's easy enough to check," Zymm said as he picked up the phone. "In fact, I'll tell them you're coming down, and you can see with your own eyes that her body is safe in storage."

Zymm talked to the medical examiner, then gave me directions to the hospital.

FIVE

THE HOSPITAL WAS only a few minutes away from the police station. Ten minutes after leaving Sergeant Zymm, I was standing in the basement of the hospital, in the morgue with Dr. Mort Weiss. He was a short, wiry guy in his forties. The lab coat he wore looked too long for him.

"Hi," he said, holding his hand out. I shook it. "So you want to see if a certain resident is still here."

I must have looked surprised because he added, "I call them residents as opposed to corpses or dead bodies. Gives them more respect." He motioned for me to come in. The morgue was chilly, and I was glad I wore a long-sleeved shirt. It was just like every movie I'd ever seen—a wall of drawers that held the bodies of the dear departed.

I'd seen dead bodies before—right after the violence and laid out in the casket at a family funeral. But I'd never seen a dead body in a morgue, which seemed even more cold and disturbing.

"I looked up Ms. Garrett's drawer number and was just about to check on the state of the body." He walked over to a drawer labeled 23, which was on the second tier. The drawer pulled out easily, and there was a reason why. There was nothing in it.

Of course, we checked every one of the drawers. I saw more corpses in various causes of death— disease, car accident, suicide, old age—in one half hour than I'd seen in my entire adult life. By the time we finished looking, I was feeling a little queasy.

Dr. Weiss looked worried. "I've never lost a resident before." He sat down and searched his computer. After a few moments, he turned to me. "I'm not sure what to do—do I call the police and tell them a corpse is missing?"

I shook my head and thought. "If Amy Garrett were still alive, and walked out on her own steam, it wouldn't be a crime, would it? But someone should be told. Since Sergeant Zymm called you, talk to him."

Weiss frowned at me. "Walked out under her own steam? What are you saying?"

I sighed. I really didn't want to get into this again. "I'm saying that several people have already seen her on campus. There is the possibility that she woke up in the drawer and found a way to get out.''

He shook his head. ''I've never had this happen before, but I've read about cases like this happening.'' He looked excited at the prospect of being written up in the *New England Medical Journal.* ''I'm not sure that a person who wakes up in one of these drawers would be able to orient herself—she wouldn't know where she was or how to get out of the drawer.''

I nodded. A weird idea formed itself in my head. I was almost hesitant to ask, but I figured Dr. Weiss had already fielded one weird request today—what was one more? ''Dr. Weiss, if you don't mind, would you let me get in one of the drawers? I want to know what it's like and if it's possible for Amy to have let herself out, providing that she figured out where she was.''

He paused, then nodded. ''I'm pretty sure a resident, if he or she woke up, wouldn't be able to open the drawer from the inside, but let's test out this theory. There's an empty one on the lower tier.'' He led me over to it. Before opening it he said, ''Just so you know, if anyone comes in, I will disavow any knowledge of your being in there.''

I nodded. ''How long can you leave me in there?''

He looked at his watch. "I can give you five minutes, then I have to get you out of there."

I got on the stainless-steel tray, no padding. Dr. Weiss insisted that I take a small penlight that he kept in his pocket. Considering that I had less time to find a way to open the drawer from the inside than Amy might have had, the penlight was welcome.

He slid the drawer in place, and I was enveloped in cold, sterile darkness. I wondered what it would be like to wake up in a drawer. Amy probably didn't feel well when she woke up, and would have been quite disoriented as to where she was.

I turned the penlight on. The drawer was roomy, but it was fortunate that I wasn't claustrophobic. Of course, I wasn't a large person, and the drawers were made for all types. From the photos I'd seen of Amy, she didn't appear to be a big person either. I slid my hand over my body and pushed on the drawer, but it didn't give. I pushed both hands against the top and tried to push my way out, but it didn't budge. I wriggled down until my feet touched the end of the drawer and tried to push off, but I didn't have enough strength. I was beginning to shiver from the cold, even with my long-sleeved shirt on. I wished I'd worn a parka instead. Amy must have been freezing as well as frightened.

I slid back into position and slowly turned over

and used the penlight to find the latch. I tried to work the latch with my fingers, but was unsuccessful. The drawer began to move, and suddenly I was back in the autopsy room, Dr. Weiss above me, a worried expression on his face.

"I was afraid to leave you in there any longer because of the cold." And the dark, I was sure.

I swung up to a seated position and got out to walk around and get some feeling back in my fingers. "There is no way she could have gotten out of there by herself."

"She didn't even have a light," Dr. Weiss pointed out. I handed him back his penlight.

"There's only one other solution," I said. Dr. Weiss met my eyes. "Someone knew she wasn't dead and came here to break her out. When was the last time you checked to make sure she was here?"

Dr. Weiss checked a logbook near the computer. "I know my colleague on the night shift has been on vacation for the last two weeks. I haven't looked in on the body since she came in, but my assistant is supposed to check on all of the residents once a day. You know, to make sure they aren't deteriorating too badly while they wait for the county forensic pathologist to come around. He's backed up, and Bristol is last on his schedule right now because we have so many empty drawers."

"Is your assistant here?"

"Sharon is on a late lunch." Dr. Weiss checked his watch. "She should be here any minute now."

I decided to wait until Sharon, the assistant, showed up. Dr. Weiss excused himself when two orderlies rolled a body into the room. He was called away for a few minutes, and I was left alone in the morgue with the tarp-covered dead body.

I retreated to his office, with his permission, and took out my cell phone to call Rosa. It was her free day for studying, and she answered after two rings.

"Hey Sis, how's everything down there?"

"Sarge! How's college life?"

"Just swell. Wanted to know how Fredd is doing without me."

"Oh, you just want to know how Fredd is doing," she teased. "Not your sister, not Ma."

I sighed. "Okay, how's Ma doing?"

"She just bought herself a trench coat."

I rolled my eyes and groaned. "Any messages?"

"Nothing that can't wait until you return."

A young woman in a white lab coat entered the morgue. She had short, dark hair that curled around her ears, and she was lean and lanky. Her name tag told me that this was Sharon.

"Gotta go work. I'll call later." I pressed the off button and put the cell phone away.

"Sharon?"

She had already noticed me, considering that I was the only body in the room who was still moving, aside from her.

"Yes?"

I introduced myself and explained my purpose for being here. She looked shocked when I told her that Amy Garrett was no longer in her box.

"That's impossible!" Sharon strode across the room, checked the roster, and opened drawer 23. "Impossible!" she said again as she closed the drawer. Then she opened the one to the right of it.

"Dr. Weiss and I have already checked every drawer. You could say we did an inventory."

Sharon turned around, blinking as if she was going to cry. Panic was evident in her face. Dr. Weiss entered the morgue and was distressed to find his assistant almost in tears.

"Sharon, please." He fluttered around her, clearly nervous around the living, who were so unpredictable.

Sharon sniffled. I retreated and got a tissue from the box on the desk.

"I don't know how this h-happened." She shook her head.

Sharon was sitting now, and I crouched down in front of her to get her attention. I explained what might have happened. She had calmed down and was giving me a skeptical look.

"That's insane. She couldn't be up and walking around."

Dr. Weiss used a gentle voice when talking to his assistant, as if she were made of fragile glass and needed special handling. "Sharon, not only is it possible, but we need to figure out how it happened. Angela has already tried to get out of the drawer by herself, and that's not possible."

I picked up from where the doc had left off. "So someone had to help her. And it happened before Friday because my client spotted her on Thursday evening."

Sharon looked away and sighed.

"Sharon, is there anything you want to tell us?"

She was trembling with fright, and she couldn't meet our eyes. "On Thursday, I worked late. Dr. Weiss left at four, but there were some autopsy tapes left to transcribe, and one autopsy report was needed for court on Friday. I left for dinner at five-thirty, and I didn't bother to lock the morgue. It was only going to take a few minutes. Twenty minutes later, I came back with my dinner, and I immediately felt as if someone had been in the morgue."

"What made you think that?" I asked.

Sharon fidgeted. "I always leave the logbook on the left side of the computer, and when I returned, it was on the right side. My chair was pushed in. I always leave it out when I get up because I usually return to it within a few minutes." She looked up briefly and shrugged, clearly embarrassed about something.

"What else, Sharon? Something else was wrong."

She paused, then added, "And drawer twenty-three wasn't closed all the way." She looked up at Dr. Weiss. "I'm sorry. I didn't check it out. I was spooked. It was late, and I told myself that it was probably some orderly playing a trick on me, or something like that. I don't like working here at night, and I decided the less I knew, the better."

Dr. Weiss looked troubled. "Why didn't you mention this to me the next day, Friday?"

"It was my day off, and the longer I waited to tell you, the more I thought it was all my imagination."

He nodded, but looked serious. "I can see how that happened."

My mind was churning out the scenario—Weiss's assistant goes to dinner, and the person who poisoned Amy Garrett sneaks in and takes Amy out of the drawer. From what I'd read, tetrodotoxin takes away the victim's freedom to think for him- or herself. The victim can function, but only on a basic level. So someone had to come in and release the drawer, and give Amy the direction she would have needed to leave the hospital.

A part of me was denying that this could have happened at all. It sounded too much like a B-movie plot. I reminded myself that zombie poison existed, and that zombies truly existed in Haiti. The difference between movie zombies and real zombies is that while they terrified characters in bad movies (they moved so slowly, you could be a mile away before they lurched two blocks), real zombies were sad soulless creatures with no ability to think for themselves.

I needed to work on the assumption that Amy had been given the zombie poison, and that she was alive, sort of. But my other questions were: Who would do such a thing and why? And where does one obtain zombie poison?

SIX

I THANKED BOTH Dr. Weiss and Sharon and left the hospital. Dr. Weiss had promised to call Sergeant Zymm and file a report of a missing corpse.

I went back to my dorm room and found that Savanna had cleaned up her half of the room. She was seated at her desk, studying. Alanis Morissette, one of my most hated singers, was playing on her CD player.

She looked up. "I'm sorry for the welcome," she said sweetly.

I was somewhat mollified. "That's okay. I suppose I'd be a little put out if some stranger came into my place and started claiming a part of my apar—room." I smiled, a way of gritting my teeth, and vowed to get to the bottom of the voodoo warnings for Dr. Cannon and of Amy Garrett's mysterious death as soon as possible so I could leave. My roommate might have had a change of heart about me, but I still didn't trust her any farther than I could throw her. I could at least try to make an effort in return.

"So why did you decide to transfer here a few weeks into the term?" she asked, appearing to be genuinely interested.

"I changed my major to forensic anthropology, and I did some research and decided to come here." I quickly went through my fake history, briefly toying with the idea of changing the country to, maybe, Korea or Luxembourg. I doubted Savanna knew her geography, but on the off chance that she remembered, I decided to stick to Poland. I hoped that Savanna didn't have relatives in Krakow. She appeared to be really interested, but I got the feeling that she was storing this information for the future. "So that's why I'm here."

Thankfully, Alanis had stopped singing. Savanna turned and put on another CD, this time Tori Amos. If there's a singer I hate more than Alanis Morissette, it's Tori. If my roommate had Fiona Apple, I'd be hiding her CDs for the rest of the time I was there.

"What about you?" I asked. "Are you an anthropology major?"

She laughed. "No, I haven't made a decision about my major yet. I'm a sophomore. I'm just getting the required courses out of the way." She looked at me slyly. "So you know Jonathan, do you?"

Now I knew what her interest in me was about. Jonathan Sharpe. She'd all but rubbed her body up against his at the end of class this morning.

"I just met him this morning," I replied. Then I pointedly added, "He lost his girlfriend recently. He took me to lunch and showed me the campus essentials."

"Yes, I heard about that girl dying." She was giving me an appraising look, as if she wasn't sure how much of a threat I might be to the goal of bagging Jonathan. If it hadn't been so far-fetched, I would have suspected her of doing away with Amy to get him. Women didn't do that to each other, did they? Of course, I had been to Filene's basement during the spring sale, and we women can get pretty vicious in order to get what we want.

I glanced at my class schedule. "Geez, I have a class in twenty minutes." In ethnobotany with Kirsten Sorenson-Andersen. Yikes. I quickly sorted through my books until I found the ethnobotany book, then I added the notebook I'd picked up for the job and my campus map, and headed out the door.

The ethnobotany class was in a large lecture hall that was in an annex to the social sciences building. The rows of chairs were in tiers that looked down on the lecturer and the blackboard, affording a view for everyone. I sat in the second row on the end. The instructor came in just on time—the students were in place, all fifty-three of us. Out of boredom, I'd counted the students who were already here and those who came in. I wouldn't stand out, and saw no need to introduce myself.

Kirsten Sorenson-Andersen was a tall, leggy, serious woman who spoke with an Oxford-educated accent. She had wire-frame glasses and kept her hair pinned up. She was a contrast in black and white, wearing crisply ironed black slacks and matching jacket with a stark white shirt underneath. As she talked about her subject, datura, which was a plant used by an Indian people of northern Mexico, the Yaquis, to experience the sensation of flight, she lit up with earnestness.

"In conclusion, datura can be administered both topically and ingested and will cause a catatonic state that can last from a few hours to a few days. Please read Section Three and think about the topic that you want to write about, then submit it to me. I'll expect you to hand in your topic by Friday."

The students began to gather up their books and papers, all one practiced move for most of the class. The guy sitting next to me wasn't in as big of a hurry, so I turned to him. "Topic?"

He was thin, with longish hair, and he struck me

as slightly older than the average college student, which immediately made me feel comfortable with him. I could see that a lot of women might think he was a nerd. He had a mop of blondish brown hair, and wore wire-rimmed glasses and a denim shirt, but there was something about him I immediately liked. I had to quell an urge to take off his glasses to see what color his eyes were.

"We have to write a fifteen-page paper on the poison of our choice," he said with a grimace. "And I thought this would be an easy course to fill my requirements." He really looked at me, possibly for the first time, then held out his hand. "Jack Wade."

"Angela Matelli. New to the class."

"Pleased to meet you."

"This isn't your major then?"

Jack shook his head. "Computers."

"Really." My interest just tripled. Not only good-looking and around my age, but in a field I could relate to. This was a guy I wanted to get to know.

"Is this your major?" he asked.

"Nope. Forensic anthropology." I consulted my class schedule again. I had a lab with Dr. Rathman at three-thirty.

"Ms. Matelli?" Kirsten Sorenson-Andersen called out. I looked down at the theatre of the lecture hall and saw her standing patiently by the blackboard.

"I'll be right there," I told her.

Jack touched my shoulder and said in a low voice, "Look, if you have the time, come on down to my computer lab at five, and I'll show you around."

I winced. "I have a lab until five-thirty, then a pizza party thrown by Dr. Cannon."

Jack nodded. "I like him. Took Anthro one-oh-one from him last term. Interesting."

I wrote my name, dorm, and room number down. "Give me a call."

He took the scrap of paper and nodded. "Great. I'll call you, and we'll go over the notes for the last few weeks of this class. I'll make copies for you."

"Ms. Matelli," the lecturer called out again, "I have your syllabus here."

I walked down the stairs to meet her. She was putting together a packet of papers.

"Sorry about that."

She ignored my apology and handed me the sheaf of papers. "You'll be able to catch up. It shouldn't be difficult. You only have two weeks to make up."

"Thanks." I stuffed the papers in the inside pocket of my notebook.

"Have you chosen a major yet?"

"Yes. Forensic anthropology. That's why I transferred to Hartmore."

She pulled her glasses down her nose to examine me. Normally, if someone looks at me the way my instructor was studying me, I ask, "What?" But I was supposed to be a student, so I couldn't be confrontational.

"Is something wrong?" I finally asked.

"No, it's just that you don't strike me as serious forensic anthropology material." I wondered if she was silently substituting the word "intelligent" for "serious."

I gave her a strange look. She was very good at insulting me without seeming to try very hard. It wasn't said in an insulting way, more like she was saying exactly what she thought—no filter there. But I suspected she knew exactly what she was saying and was looking for a specific reaction. Instead of responding to her, I waited her out.

It worked. She finally waved me off like Queen Elizabeth dismissing one of her subjects. "We're through. You may go."

I looked at my watch. "Oh. Well, I have to be at my lab with Dr. Rathman. I'm not sure where it's located."

"Dr. Rathman's lab is in the next building. We call it the da Vinci building. In the basement."

I turned and ran as fast as I could, arriving at

Rathman's lab just a few minutes late. There were already half a dozen students there, all serious about studying human anatomy.

Rathman was a portly, balding little man with glasses. He wore a white lab coat, although it hardly seemed necessary. He glanced at me as I slipped into the lab, then went on with his lecture. The other students didn't even turn around to see who had entered the back of the lab.

"Today we're going to concentrate on the eyes," Rathman announced.

I noted that a skull sat in front of every student, and slabs of clay were nearby as well. Each skull was fixed on a stand. Clay had been applied to each skull.

I stood there feeling like I wasn't wearing any clothes. I hadn't a clue what to do. I sat on a stool at the nearest empty lab table and waited. Once Rathman set up the other students and answered their questions, they began working on their sculpting skills. Dr. Rathman turned his attention to me.

"You're new?" he said.

I handed him my registration. He looked it over and nodded. "Angela Matelli, right?"

"Right."

"We just started working on the skulls last week, so you don't have much catching up to do. In fact, we can catch up with one intensive hour, if you can stay after to set up a time.''

"Sure.''

''We'll have to set you up with a skull and clay right now. The skulls are in the box over there.'' He pointed to a box in an open closet.

"Are they…real?'' I couldn't help asking him.

He smiled a much nicer smile than Kirsten Sorenson-Andersen's, and even giggled a little. ''You know, that's what most of the students ask. But no, they're plastic. We wouldn't start you out on real skulls. But they are casts from real skulls. We use several different types so that no two skulls are alike when we finish at the end of the term.'' He gestured to the closet. ''So go get yourself a nice plastic one, and I'll start you out with some clay. After class, we can go back to my office and get you a syllabus, and you can catch up on your reading.''

I figured that would give me plenty of time to talk to him alone about Amy Garrett.

During the next two hours, we were instructed on how to sculpt eye sockets and eyebrows. He let the class go early after they put their skulls away— no one stayed after to ask any questions, and no one gave me a second glance as the new student.

''Well, Ms. Matelli,'' he said as he gathered up

his papers, "let's go back to my office for a moment, and I'll find that syllabus."

His office was on the second floor in the physical science building across the street. He found the class outline and handed it to me. "Would you be able to come in at eight tomorrow morning for an hour in the lab? I don't have a class until nine."

I consulted my schedule—I couldn't believe I was even doing that. So what if I missed a class, right? Eight was fine, I told him before I left.

SEVEN

I ARRIVED AT Dr. Cannon's office at 5:45, and he was waiting. Jonathan came in a few minutes later, and Kirsten knocked on the open door at almost six o'clock. She seemed surprised to see me there.

"I didn't know that you were acquainted with Dr. Cannon, Ms. Matelli," she said. She'd taken her glasses off, and her hair was in a French braid. A casual khaki A-line skirt and a pale blue-and-white-striped blouse had replaced her severe black-and-white suit. Her face was scrubbed of any makeup, and she gave me a killer smile.

I raised my eyebrows in surprise. The woman who had given the lecture earlier today was a completely different person from the one who was standing in front of me now. Good twin—evil twin.

"Dr. Cannon is my adviser," I explained. "And please don't worry about this afternoon."

"No offense, Angela, but Dr. Cannon," Jonathan turned to him, "why are we throwing this welcome party for her? You have a lot of students, and her major is forensic anthropology, not cultural anthropology."

"She's helping me with some research for a book," Cannon explained.

I thought it was a good explanation, until I noticed that Jonathan looked horrified. I tried not to look surprised. Dr. Cannon was elaborating on our relationship—and that was never good after you've worked on a cover story. It just gave me more details to have to remember and keep straight.

Jonathan looked stricken. "I—I just thought that when it came time to work on your book, you'd ask me to help."

I saved my client from embarrassment. "I—I think Dr. Cannon wants you to do more of the editing and some of the writing. I'm just doing the boring parts. He knew I needed a job," I glanced at Dr. Cannon, who nodded imperceptibly, "you know, just to earn a little extra money, and this came along at the right time for me. I didn't mean to tread on any toes here." I looked straight at Jonathan, and after holding my look for a moment, he grinned, nodded, and put his arm around my shoulders in a friendly manner.

"Let's go get some pizza." I looked back at Dr. Cannon, who wore a relieved expression as he turned and locked the office door.

Cannon drove all of us in his Dakota to a pizza

joint run by a real Italian family called Domenico.
The pizza joint was dark, with laminated tables and
beat-up chairs. Chianti bottles with dried flowers
tucked in them sat on the tables as a form of dec-
oration. I felt right at home. One of the places in
East Boston that I already missed was Santarpio's
Pizza. I was a regular customer there, ordering a
pizza or their marinated lamb at least once a week.

Domenico's pizza was similar to Santarpio's. If
this case went on too long and I got homesick, it
was nice to know I could come down here for a
taste of East Boston.

We talked about various things—Cannon and
Kirsten sat on one side of the table; Jonathan and I
shared the other side. Our pizza had just arrived
when another person entered Domenico's and Cannon waved him over. Dreadlocks sprouted from his
skull-like head. He was dark skinned and slender.
He was beautiful to look at.

"Simon, join us," Jonathan called out.

Simon looked over and smiled. "Hey, good to
see you again, Jonathan." He had a Caribbean accent. He strolled over and pulled up a chair.

I sat across from Kirsten. I noticed that her color
was higher than usual, and there was something in
her eyes—that look women have when they're interested in a man.

Simon had taken notice of me, the new person in the group.

Dr. Cannon spoke up. "Angela, this is Simon Lynch. He's got a grant to teach here at Hartmore for a year. Simon, Angela Matelli."

He stuck out his hand and shook mine. I felt an electric tingle run down my arm. I never wanted to let go. He had a magnetism that was intoxicating.

"What do you teach?" I asked.

"Art." I was suddenly very interested in art.

"My little sister is an art history major. She's graduating in May."

"Simon is a well-known artist back in Haiti. His work is just now being discovered here in the States," Cannon told me.

"What kind of media do you use?"

"Mixed."

"He uses collage and acrylic paint," Kirsten said, her sparkling eyes glued to him and her face a light shade of pink.

He grinned, showing beautiful white teeth. "Kirsten is my biggest fan." Hmm. A mutual admiration society.

"Simon has a gallery showing here at the college," Dr. Cannon said. "In fact, I think the opening is tomorrow night for the faculty and specially invited guests."

"I'd love to see your work," I told Simon.

"Well, then, why don't you come as my special guest?" Simon said. "Feel free to bring a guest of your own."

"Thank you," I replied. "I will." It would give me a chance to pick Simon's brains about Haiti and zombies and, um, whatever. I tried to concentrate on my job and not think about the attractive man seated next to me. I could feel Kirsten shooting daggers at me. She was clearly very possessive of him. Simon didn't seem to notice, but I suspected he secretly knew and was delighted by the possibility of having two women interested in him.

We ate the large pizzas that had been cooling for the last few minutes, and everyone had advice for me about Hartmore—the professors to avoid, the places I just had to visit.

I decided to change the subject. "What's with that girl Savanna?" I asked Jonathan. I noticed Kirsten looked uncomfortable at the mention of Savanna's name, and I wondered why.

He laughed. "She's like a lot of the other freshman and sophomore girls. Their hormones are in charge rather than their brains." He turned to the others and explained how he had walked in on what might have turned into a girl fight.

"I don't think many men would turn down the chance to watch a girl fight," Simon said with a grin. He turned to look at Kirsten, who was careful to look nonchalant.

I shook my head. "I suppose I was like that when I first attended college." I was pretty sure I hadn't been like that, but I was in a forgiving mood.

Simon finished his drink and stood. "Well, I have to get back to the gallery. There are still works to hang." He said his good-byes and left.

The discussion went back to my roommate.

"You were saying earlier that you were like Savanna at one time," Kirsten said. "I think of myself as a good judge of character, and I don't see that quality in you."

I shrugged, uncomfortable that the focus was on me. "People change. Young girls go through an awkward phase, and their self-esteem becomes wrapped up in how they affect men."

"That's so true," Kirsten replied. "But you appear to be very…confident. You seem more mature than some of the doctoral students." I couldn't have been more uncomfortable if Kirsten had been interrogating me in a German accent and I was seated in a kitchen chair under a single seventy-five-watt bulb in a darkened room.

Dr. Cannon picked up the gauntlet. "Angela is an ex-Marine."

"No such thing as an ex-Marine," I quipped.

"Ah, that may explain it." Kirsten seemed to think about it.

"Who were you thinking of when you mentioned other female doctoral students?" Jonathan asked. There was tension in his voice, and, not for the first time since we'd been sitting at Domenico's, I got the feeling that Jonathan and Kirsten didn't like each other.

"Sometimes I think Amy could have used a little more self-esteem. I don't mean to be insulting, Jonathan, but she was very dependent."

I was surprised that she brought up Amy—Jonathan was clearly still grieving, but Kirsten had earlier shown a penchant for playing devil's advocate.

Jonathan leaned forward. "What do you mean by that?" He didn't sound happy.

Kirsten looked down and shrugged. "She gave up a very good job offer to stay here until you graduated. Maybe if she had taken that job, she would still be alive."

I managed to keep quiet.

Jonathan leaned closer to Kirsten. "And maybe if you and I had stayed together, my antidote wouldn't be missing. Is that what you're really saying?"

Kirsten stared straight back at him. Her jaw was tight when she spoke again. "I've told you before, and I'm telling you now, that I don't have your antidote. If I did, I'd be applying for grants to develop it right now.''

"And I'd be suing you." The words were becoming heated and no longer involved Amy. "Of course, I recently discovered that you *have* applied for a grant.''

Kirsten set her jaw. "To go back to Haiti and research folk remedies. Why would I do that if I had your stupid formula?''

"Because you're smart enough to want to make it look like *you* discovered the formula rather than me.''

Her voice got quiet—the sound of tight anger. "And you think that Amy wasn't interested in you solely because of your formula?''

Jonathan paled, then became sullen. He stood up abruptly and turned to Dr. Cannon. "I think I'd better leave before I say something I might regret.'' I thought Jonathan and Kirsten had both said plenty that they might regret. Jonathan nodded shortly in my direction and, ignoring Kirsten, left. I gave a little wave to his back. Dr. Cannon was staring at his Pepsi as if it might get up and do a lap dance or something.

When enough silence had passed, Dr. Cannon leaned back and took his glasses off to clean them. "Well, Kirsten, you've done it again.''

"Done what, Doctor?" She looked cool and collected. It was hard for me to swallow that she had no idea of what she was doing. It was almost as if she was trying to clear us out by insulting us so she could be alone with Dr. Cannon. But I didn't get the feeling she was attracted to him. It seemed to be more of a power thing with her.

Dr. Cannon sighed and shook his head. "You need a class or two in how to be a human being. There's no point in explaining what you did. I think you are perfectly aware of your actions." He stood up and looked at me. "I'm sorry for this embarrassing display, Angela. Would you like a ride back to campus?"

I smiled. "Thanks, Doc. I think I'll stay a little longer and walk back. You forget—I'm Italian. This is nothing compared to some of the family disagreements I've witnessed!" I grinned and, turning slightly away from Kirsten, winked at him. Actually, I was furious with him because the antidote thing seemed to be something of a clue to why Amy might have been fed zombie poison.

He suppressed a smile. "I'll see you tomorrow, early, Angela. I need to go over some of the research with you. I've found more sources."

"I have a makeup lab with Dr. Rathman at eight." I thought it would be a good opportunity to talk to him about his impression of Amy.

"Come to my office when you're through. I don't have a class until ten-thirty."

If I hadn't decided that talking to Kirsten alone might turn up some useful information, I would have taken him up on his offer to get a ride back to campus. Instead, I nodded, and he left. Kirsten was toying with the straw in her drink. She cocked her head and looked at me. "Why are you really here?"

I was beginning to think that she had some kind of sixth sense, but I reminded myself that devil's advocates love to worry a subject to death. I acted as if her underlying suspicions didn't bother me, and I turned the subject around to her.

"I'm just watching a master of manipulation. What's in it for you when you alienate everyone in the anthropology department?"

She shrugged. "They're not everyone. I don't need them." She looked straight at me. "But I don't understand your role here at Hartmore. I get the feeling there's more to you than meets the eye."

I crossed my arms and, with a smile, slumped down in my seat. I got the feeling that my casual attitude bothered Kirsten, and that gave me some satisfaction. "I'm a transfer student. Isn't that sufficient? Why the interrogation?"

It took her a moment to decide, then she nodded to herself, as if she'd been arguing whether to be honest. "I saw you coming out of the police station yesterday in the early afternoon. I didn't put it together when I saw you at my lecture earlier today, but seeing you outside of the college environment reminded me."

"So, you think I might be on parole or probation or, better yet, I'm undercover for some reason." Hitting close to the truth and being on the offensive made Kirsten back off.

"I didn't mean it that way." The devil's advocate was now on the defensive.

"What way did you mean it?"

She had been frowning, but now she smiled as if realizing that I had turned the tables on her. "Well, the fact that you are suddenly here and working for Don bothers me. Jonathan and I usually know everything Dr. Cannon does before he does it. He discusses every decision he makes that may affect the projects we work on together." She gestured to me. "But you appear here at the college out of the blue, and are suddenly working for Don without either of us knowing anything until now. And you're majoring in forensic anthropology just like Amy Garrett. It's too much of a coincidence."

And she and Jonathan were so close to Dr. Cannon and each other. She had a point—I wished that Dr. Cannon had been able to make my major something a little different, but it was the only way I

could talk to some of the professors who were
Amy's instructors.

"I can change my major, if it would make you
more comfortable."

Her eyes twinkled. She was such an odd mixture
of devil's advocate and biting cynicism. I kind of
liked her, but she was prickly to be around. "That
won't be necessary. You've somehow managed to
avoid explaining why you were at the police station."

"I dropped in there to visit with a friend of a
friend," I explained, leaving out the extra "of a
friend." "And the reason Dr. Cannon didn't say
anything is that my transfer was pretty abrupt."

A light went on in her eyes. "Ah, the trouble in
Poland."

I didn't disabuse her of that notion. "Since I've
declared forensic anthropology, would you mind
telling me about Amy? Her death was a tragic
loss."

Her suspicious eyes searched me. "Why do you
want to know anything about her?"

"Well, you and Jonathan really had a go-around
about her. Dr. Cannon did call her death mysterious. Very odd, don't you think? No apparent cause.
A perfectly healthy woman dies after a short illness
that simulates the flu." I shook my head. "What a
shame." I wondered what she'd say if I told her

that I'd been to the morgue and Amy's body, for all intents and purposes, had just gotten up and walked away. But it wasn't information I felt I could share.

Kirsten took a sip of her diet soda. "A tragedy."

I leaned forward. "You don't strike me as very sincere. I know you and Jonathan don't get along, but the man just lost the woman he loved. Do you honestly think Amy might have stolen the formula?"

Kirsten frowned. "No, I don't. I just said that to get a rise out of him. He's had it in for me ever since the antidote went missing. We used to date. I broke up with him about the same time that the antidote disappeared."

"Did you?"

"Did I what—take the formula?" She thought about it. "No, I didn't. You know, Jonathan isn't the only one who has lived in Haiti. I spent a good deal of my childhood there. I could go back and talk to a number of people I know, and find someone who would give me a formula that might or might not be an antidote to tetrodotoxin." She shrugged. "Several tests have already been done on the formula, and they all came back inconclusive."

"So you're saying that Jonathan's formula hadn't been tested much before it disappeared."

"That's right. And Amy came into his life about

the same time I was leaving. She could easily have taken it." She paused, seeming to realize she sounded shrewish. "Please don't get me wrong about Amy. I liked her well enough, but Jonathan wasn't right for her."

"Wasn't that their business?"

She took a sip from her glass of diet soda.

"It must have been difficult to see them together."

Kirsten smiled, but there was no warmth there. "Not really. I broke it off with him. We had very little in common other than similar majors and the fact that we both lived in Haiti for a time. I'm seeing Simon now."

I nodded, tucking away that bit of information about Jonathan. "How interesting. How did you end up living in Haiti?"

She ran her fingers through her hair. "My father and mother were missionaries. My half sister and I grew up there."

"Did you meet any practicing *houngans*?"

She looked slightly troubled, but finally answered my question. "Of course. They attended our services every Sunday." I had the feeling that she was being evasive.

I raised my eyebrows.

"The Haitians see no problem with being good Christians and hedging their bets by also practicing their *vodoun* beliefs. It's not uncommon in Third World countries where good Christian folk decide to invade the culture and offer the *right* religion to the poor heathens."

"You sound as if you almost detest the idea of missionary work." She sounded very harsh when she talked about religion. But then, Kirsten had set herself up as a cynic, and I doubted she believed in anything other than cold, hard facts.

Kirsten stood up. "My half sister and I saw enough of how our parents treated the Haitians— like they were poor primitive heathens, sheep who needed to be herded in the right direction to save their souls." She gave a sharp laugh. "The funny thing about their type of Christianity is that there was this paradox going on in their logic: the missionaries want to save souls in places like Haiti, but they don't believe that these people have souls to save." She laughed and shook her head.

I got up, and we left Domenico's and headed back toward the campus.

I agreed with her that there were missionaries who felt that way; there were also missionaries who didn't preach in that way and who did treat everyone with respect. "What did your parents teach the Haitians?" I asked.

"They taught 'the unwashed,' as they liked to call the Haitians, about Jesus and how to be pious and turn the other cheek. They frowned on the ideas of keeping voodoo beliefs, standing up for oneself, and standing up for what is right.''

"The meek shall inherit the earth."

Kirsten laughed. "The meek shall get trampled over by the good Christian bullies—that's the real story."

I didn't believe it for a minute—but I didn't want to argue with her.

It had gotten dark, and the town of Bristol had rolled up its sidewalks, other than the bars that were still open.

"You must have had some encounters with voodoo," I said.

There was a pause before she answered—again, the evasion. "Yes, we did. Some of the Haitian people resented our presence and left gifts on our doorstep to scare us."

"Like voodoo dolls and chicken hearts?"

"More like fresh cow dung."

I laughed. "Sorry. I'm sure it was traumatic at the time."

"For my parents. I was fascinated."

"Is that what led you to your specialization?"

She nodded. "We had a Haitian nanny, Cecile, who used to take me on Fridays to visit her grandmother in the outskirts of Port-au-Prince. Her grandmother was a medicine woman and taught me how to use many of the herbs around the island.''

I filed that information away for later. Of course, it wasn't anything new that Kirsten had knowledge of toxic plants. She taught a course in ethnobotany. But that, combined with the fact that she was Jonathan's ex-girlfriend, made me wonder if there was something to Amy's death other than senseless tragedy.

As we crossed the street to enter the campus, Kirsten froze and gave a little cry of surprise.

''What's wrong?'' I asked.

''Do you see that girl over there?'' She pointed beyond a big sign that announced to the world that it was about to enter Hartmore College. A figure slowly stepped into a pool of light from the sign. The lighting made the figure, a girl, look spooky. But even in that light, it was clear that there was something odd about her. There was a dullness, a lethargy, in the way she conducted herself.

It was as if someone were controlling her with a remote. I was only dimly aware at the time that this was my first encounter with a zombie.

EIGHT

IF I HADN'T witnessed the whole thing, I wouldn't have believed it.

After we spotted the figure of the woman across the street, I had to hold Kirsten back from running across the street while the light was red. Good thing, too, because a Mack truck careened around the corner just at the last moment and would have mowed her down before she reached the other side.

When the street was clear again, we hurried over there, and searched the area.

"What are we searching for?" I finally asked her as I straightened up from looking around a fir tree.

"Amy Garrett. I could have sworn that was Amy Garrett." Kirsten looked pale and strained in the dark.

A chill ran up my spine as fast and light as a hummingbird. My laugh sounded high and unnatural. "I'm sure it was just some college student who looks like her." More like some homeless schizo. Whoever we had seen looked like the life had been burned out of her.

Kirsten didn't look convinced, but we headed back to the dorms.

She lingered outside my dorm. "I need to go to the library."

"Will you be all right?" I asked. I had more questions to ask her, but now didn't seem to be the time.

The walk must have done her good. Her color had come back, and she gave me her superior smile. "Of course I'll be fine."

Before she could leave, I tried one more time. "Kirsten—"

She raised her eyebrows, now back to her aloof manner.

"Is something going on that I don't know about?"

"What do you mean?"

"I just get the feeling that there was more to your animosity toward Jonathan."

She laughed in a way that would have made a less confident person feel like a complete fool for asking such a stupid question. "Nothing beyond what you witnessed earlier." She turned to me again. "Look, Angela, please don't get the wrong idea. You and I are *not* going to be fast friends over the incident that just happened. And if you bring it up to anyone else, I will *deny* that it happened." She took out a cigarette and lit it. I noticed that her hand was shaking and that it took two swipes with the Bic lighter to light it.

"I have no reason to bring up the subject of seeing a ghost to anyone," I said as reasonably as possible. "They would all think I was nuts. And I have no intention of thinking about you as a friend."

She disappeared into the darkness until all I could see was the glow of her cigarette whenever she inhaled. I wondered what demons she had encountered in her lifetime to make her such a contradiction.

I didn't go into my dorm immediately. I went instead to Dr. Cannon's home a few blocks away. His Dakota was in the driveway, so I knew he was home.

I knocked on his door, and it took a few minutes for him to answer. When he did, the doctor didn't look well.

"Angela. You got here pretty quickly." It was after ten o'clock. He seemed to realize that I had no idea what he was talking about.

I was confused. "What do you mean?"

He looked shaken. "Didn't you get my message?"

It dawned on me. "You must have left a message at my dorm."

He nodded. I didn't tell him that Savanna probably wouldn't get the message to me. "I haven't been back there yet."

He stepped aside and let me in. Once inside the house, I looked at him again and saw how pale he was.

"You don't look so hot," I said.

"I'm very tired."

"I saw Amy. At least, I think I saw Amy. Kirsten was with me, and she swore it was Amy. Then she told me not to tell anyone. Like anyone but you'd believe me." I told him about my meeting with Sergeant Zymm, and how I'd mentioned the possibility of Amy being alive, and about going to the morgue and confirming that her body was no longer there.

"And I received another warning." He showed me a box of shriveled roses that was lying on his coffee table. There was no card, no florist name on the box. I didn't touch it with my fingers, just with a tissue provided by my client.

"How much have you touched this box?"

"Just to open it," he said. "I didn't know it was another warning."

"Have you called the police?"

"Not yet." He paced. "I'm gonna be honest with you, Angela. I'm getting pretty spooked. Why would someone want to send me these warnings? What have I done?"

"Dr. Cannon, you saw Amy, or you thought you saw Amy, the night after she died. Doesn't that tell you something?"

He nodded. "Yeah. But why not come right out and say it—send me one of those messages made from cut-up newspapers and magazines?"

"You spent time in Haiti. He or she is trying to tell you in a way that will scare you into silence. But it ended up looking like a joke to you at first. I'm afraid the next move may be to shut you up permanently. Is there any place you can go? Can you take time out from your schedule?"

He stroked his beard thoughtfully. "I have classes, Angela. I can't just up and leave."

I ran a hand through my hair. "Okay. But be careful. And if you see anything out of the ordinary, anything that may spell trouble for you, I want you to run. Go somewhere, get out of here for a while." I gave him my cell phone number. "Call me if you feel you're in danger."

I picked up the phone and called the police. Sergeant Zymm was off duty, the dispatcher said, but she would send the first available car out to Dr. Cannon's house.

While we waited for a policeman to respond, Cannon asked, "You must have come here for something if you didn't respond to my message. What can I do for you?''

"Do you have a picture of Amy Garrett?"

He frowned for a moment. "Wait. I know we had pictures taken last spring at a faculty picnic." He disappeared into what I presumed to be his bedroom, and returned a few moments later carrying a shoe box full of pictures.

After sorting through the photo envelopes, he pulled out a photo and handed it to me. Jonathan and a girl with short, dark red hair were sharing a piece of watermelon and laughing. Watermelon juice was running down Jonathan's chin, and the girl, Amy, was trying to wipe it off with a paper napkin.

A second picture showed Jonathan and Amy grinning at the camera, heads touching, his arm around her shoulders. She was small boned—probably best described as elfin—and wore intricate beaded dangling earrings and a dark red sleeveless T-shirt that highlighted sculpted shoulders and tan shorts that showed off her sleek, compact legs. She had big, warm brown eyes and straight white teeth. Amy wore no makeup.

I studied the photos and compared the woman in them to the woman Kirsten and I had spotted from across the street. It could be the same person.

"I should have shown you these photos the other night when you arrived," he said apologetically.

"That's okay, I should have asked. If I hadn't been so tired from the trip up here, I might have thought of it."

He let out a sigh. "Then I guess it is possible that she's still alive."

"Now I have to find her," I said. "Is there a possibility that she might have gone back home?"

He looked troubled. "How much have you read of the zombie victim?"

I shook my head. "You tell me."

"Because tetrodotoxin affects the nervous system, deadening it, the victim descends into a comalike state." He looked at me and nodded. "This much we know."

"We can't be certain that's what happened to Amy, but so far it seems like the best educated guess."

"From there, the victim eventually regains some movement, although he or she would be virtually trapped in a body with no verbal or cognitive abilities."

"So you're saying that once Amy woke up in the morgue drawer, she wouldn't have been able to think of a way out of the situation." Like banging on the door or yelling.

"No."

"She would have had to wait for someone to open the drawer."

He nodded.

"Dr. Cannon, I'm not even sure what I'm investigating at this point. We have a girl who supposedly died, but who has been seen around campus by you, and as of this evening, by Kirsten and myself. And then we have a bunch of, for lack of a better term, tasteless practical jokes that have been played on you." And I remembered one other thing that was recently mentioned. "And now I find out that there's this tetrodotoxin antidote that's been stolen."

Dr. Cannon shook his head. "I'm sorry. I didn't think it had anything to do with me."

"Okay, tell me your thoughts on the subject of the antidote. Do you think it could work?"

"I know there are many forms of antidotes all over Haiti. Every *bokor,* every *bizango* society, has its own version. There doesn't even seem to be a pattern of ingredients. Frankly, the reason I didn't mention it to you is that I don't think there's anything to it. Amy didn't think so either."

My ears perked up. "Really? Amy didn't think there was anything to the antidote?"

"That was the one thing Jonathan and Amy didn't agree on."

Aha. So all hadn't been well in paradise. "Did they fight about it?"

Dr. Cannon shrugged. "Not really fighting exactly, more like disagreeing. They didn't come to blows, and there really wasn't any yelling—at least not in my presence. Amy confided in me that she suspected that Jonathan's 'cure' wasn't everything he thinks it is."

"How did he come by the antidote?" I asked, curious about why Jonathan would put such stock in this particular formula.

Cannon stroked his beard thoughtfully. "Jonathan once told me that he got the formula while he was working there for the Peace Corps. He had seen the antidote work on several people who had been poisoned."

I would have to ask Jonathan more about his antidote.

"What was the form? Was it a list of ingredients on paper?"

He shook his head. "No. I believe he had a vial of it stored in his freezer. He was planning to have it analyzed for content and percentages."

"Do you know if he had a chemist lined up?"

"Someone in the chemistry department, I think. I don't know any names."

Another idea struck me. "Did you ever think that maybe the warnings were being sent to you by Jonathan? Maybe he thinks you stole it, or that you were in on it with Kirsten Sorenson-Andersen?''

He ran a hand over the back of his neck. ''It hadn't even occurred to me. I had no idea I'd given you such a big job.''

I immediately felt guilty and started to back-pedal. ''Sorry for dropping this all on you.''

''How did you like your first day in college?''

I grinned. ''Hectic. Odd.'' I told him about spotting the woman who looked like Amy, according to Kirsten. ''What's with Kirsten, anyway? Does she have a good twin and an evil twin? She seems to be all over the place.''

''She came here on a grant about nine months ago, and I think she has an extension to stay another term.''

''How long ago was the formula found missing?''

''Jonathan and Kirsten stopped dating four months ago. He immediately began dating Amy, may even have been seeing her secretly until Kirsten broke up with him.''

A woman scorned…I thought. Could she be involved in Amy's ''death''? When Amy appeared earlier tonight, Kirsten appeared to be as startled as I was.

''Of course, when the accusations began to fly, Amy took Jonathan's side,'' I said.

He nodded. "Yes."

"What about you? Where do you stand?"

He grinned. "Firmly on the sidelines."

I was beginning to see a glimmer of—something? I wasn't sure of what, but the antidote seemed to have something to do with what had happened to Amy.

There was a knock at the door. Dr. Cannon answered it, and a uniformed policeman stepped inside. The cop looked like he was twelve years old—even his uniform looked like it was too big for him.

The report only took about ten minutes—there wasn't much for Dr. Cannon to tell, and very little the uniformed policeman could do, other than take notes and inspect the box and flowers.

NINE

I DIDN'T GET MUCH sleep that night—maybe four hours. When I crept into my room at three in the morning, Savanna was sprawled across her bed. Her computer was running a screensaver program—hunky male models in various states of undress. Savanna herself was wearing a tiny strappy T-shirt and bikini underwear. Apparently that was comfortable sleepwear for her. If I'd been wearing that, I'd be pulling at everything, so that it didn't cling to my body like wet dental floss. I tiptoed to my bed and stripped down, slipping into a large T-shirt that I'd left out on the bed.

As I slipped between the covers, Savanna said, "Some guy called you. Started with a *J*."

"Jonathan?"

Her voice was sleepy, but I could hear the frost on the edge of her voice. "No, not him. Someone else."

I was sleepy, but my mind drifted through the day until I said, "Jack?"

"Mmm-hmm," was all I got from her.

I WAS UP at seven. I'm not good at functioning on less than eight hours' sleep, but I was working, and I couldn't just take a day off.

I reviewed what I'd learned yesterday: Amy was missing from her drawer at the morgue, Kirsten and I had spied her romping near the entrance to Hartmore College, and apparently there was a missing antidote to the zombie poison.

I realized that I would need to find out more about the antidote. I needed to get into Amy's house and search it for zombie poison, and I had to look for Amy. I wasn't sure how I was going to get into her place unless I confessed my real purpose in being here at Hartmore to Jonathan, but even then, I couldn't be sure he would allow me to search the house. Letting him in on my undercover work might do more harm than good. Besides, I would have to talk to my client before revealing my real purpose here to anyone.

I stumbled around and got dressed without so much as splashing water on my face, grabbed the items I needed, and headed out the door, leaving my roommate to imitate Sleeping Beauty.

When I got to the Student Union, I went to the bank of telephones and called Rosa.

"Hello?" she croaked.

"It's me."

"Sarge. What's up?"

"Me, and you, as soon as you have your coffee. Look, I need you to get in touch with Antonia." I hoped she could get some background checks done for me very quickly. I gave Rosa the names: Kirsten Sorenson-Andersen, Simon Lynch, Jonathan Sharpe, Amy Garrett.

"I'll probably have other names to add to the list, but it's a start."

"I'll try to reach Antonia right away, Sarge," Rosa promised.

I thanked her and hung up.

After picking up a muffin and a Starbucks coffee to go at the Wild Onion, I headed straight over to Dr. Rathman's lab in the da Vinci building across campus. He was already there, setting my skull up.

"Good morning, Ms. Matelli," he chirped.

I tried to return the greeting, but it came out as "uhhh."

He looked me over. "You look like you didn't get a very good night's sleep. Too much partying, most likely." He turned back to the lab table. "My first impression of you was wrong."

"What do you mean?" I managed to ask.

"My first impression was that you were more mature than the average student." What was it about me—maybe there was a neon sign on my forehead that told everyone I was older than the average student? I always prided myself on being able to get away with looking younger than my almost thirty years. "Most students spend their first year partying, then about fifty percent of them settle down to study."

"What happens to the other fifty percent?"

"They either drop out or they limp along until their grades become so bad that the college gives them an ultimatum—shape up and ship out."

"What category was Amy Garrett in?"

Dr. Rathman stopped what he was doing and adjusted his glasses. "Amy? She was a straight-A student, a natural for forensic anthropology. Her computer background helped." He looked at me over the top of his glasses. "Why do you ask?"

I shrugged. "Just curious." I looked away from him, studying my skull. I needed to talk about Amy and get his impressions of her death. "I understand Amy had flu symptoms before she died. Has it been going around?"

Dr. Rathman frowned. "I don't know much about how she died. I only know that her death was a shock to everyone who knew her. I don't know anything about a flu going around campus. Not yet, anyway. It usually takes another month to hit— around the time of midterms." There was a twinkle in his eye, and I chuckled along with him.

Then we moved on to the skull in front of me. As he lectured me on the structure of the skull and the differences between male and female, he lost track of his thought more than once. I wondered how shaken he was by what I'd told him, and how much he was just being a stereotypical absent-minded professor.

The hour went by quickly. At the end, he told me we had pretty much caught up to where the class was now. My skull had the clay molded around it and was looking pretty good.

"You're a quick learner," he told me as we walked out. "Thanks. Tell me a little bit about Amy. Was she going to be a good forensic anthropologist?"

He nodded. "She had the potential to be at the top of her field. She was training to specialize in working with the computer rather than in sculpting, although forensic anthropologists need to have both skills. I think she was planning to work mainly with the FBI, concentrating on victims of serial killers. The week before she died, Amy told me that she had applied and was scheduled for an interview at Quantico."

That was interesting. No one had mentioned Amy had applied to the FBI—could it be that she hadn't told Jonathan, and Dr. Cannon didn't know because she didn't want Jonathan to know? Could it be that all had not been well in paradise?

I checked my class schedule—if I attended all of my classes, I'd never get any investigating done. Fortunately, it was a time-honored tradition for college students to skip the occasional class. I would just have to skip all of my classes. There was a class in philosophy and one in chemistry coming up. I didn't need to go to those classes. I wavered about the chemistry class, but decided that I could go to the next one if I found the tetrodotoxin, and have the professor analyze it for me, if necessary. I headed for my Bronco.

"Angela, wait up!" I turned and saw Jack Wade heading toward me.

"Sorry I didn't get back in touch," I told him. "I got your message about three this morning." Ouch. That sounded bad, like I was a slut or something. Then I realized I was at a college and getting in at three in the morning wasn't shocking because most people would assume you were studying until then.

He raised his eyebrows. "Wanna go someplace and talk?"

I really needed to figure out how to get into Amy's house.

"I have an appointment right now, but can we meet later today?"

He nodded. "I'm free till two."

We agreed to meet at the Wild Onion at eleven-thirty. That would give me time to visit with Cannon in his office, and if I had the time, I'd find Amy Garrett's place and check it out. I didn't have any idea where she lived, and I couldn't ask Jonathan. I'd have to talk to Cannon about it.

Jack said good-bye, and I walked to Cannon's office. The weather was beautiful, a crisp fall day—cool but sunny. The leaves were turning bright colors, and some had fallen to the ground, creating a crunchy brown carpet under my feet as I walked back to the social sciences building.

Dr. Cannon's office door was ajar, and Jonathan was inside, sitting at his desk. He looked up when I stood in the doorway. "Angela. You looking for the doc?"

I nodded. "Yeah, I had a couple of questions for him."

"He's at a department meeting. Sorry about last night. I left kind of abruptly."

I chuckled. "Gee, I can't imagine why—"

His smile was hesitant, but he finally relented and even laughed quietly. "I'm glad you understand."

"I understand you once lived in Haiti."

He nodded. "I was a Peace Corps volunteer for two years. I plan to go back after I get my degree."

"Was Amy going with you?"

He blinked. "No. Actually, these are recent plans. I decided that after I graduate I'll go back there." He shook his head. "I had plans to marry Amy, have a family, a good job, the whole nine yards." He clasped his hands in front, his elbows resting on the arms of the chair. "That dream is dead. I'll go back where I belong."

"Was Amy aware that you wanted to marry her? Was she like-minded?"

He gave me a strange look. "Of course she was."

"So you'll be going back to Haiti. Is that how you became interested in anthropology? Your work in Haiti?"

He nodded. "I got to know an ethnobotanist while I was working in a small village, and I often helped him gather samples of plants. I just became fascinated with the relationship among the plants and the people and their belief system."

I nodded. "I understand that's what drove Kirsten Sorenson-Andersen as well."

He stiffened. "Yes, I suppose it did."

It seemed to be the time to bring it up. "Dr. Cannon mentioned to me the other day that you two dated briefly."

"Long enough for her to steal the antidote to tetrodotoxin that I possessed," he said in an uncharitable tone.

"Can't you bring an action against her?"

He tapped a pen. "I can't prove she has it, and I can't prove I originally had it if she takes it to a pharmaceutical company."

A thought occurred to me. "If she has it, she has to take it somewhere to have it tested. Wouldn't it be easier to take it to someone in Hartmore's chemistry department?"

His eyes lit up briefly. "Maybe. I don't know." He laughed, but there was no humor there. "You met her last night. What do you think?"

I told him I thought that Kirsten Sorenson-Andersen was a study in contradictions. And I thought that she wasn't about to give up anything she acquired through either hard work or deception. The jury was still out about Jonathan Sharpe.

"She swears she had nothing to do with its disappearance," Jonathan continued. "I've been working on recreating it, but without the list, I've been unable to get my ingredients to work."

"But you're not an ethnobotanist," I pointed out.

He nodded. "True, but my master's thesis was on linking the flora of Haiti to the culture."

"Well, I hope you find it." I crossed my arms and sat on the corner of Cannon's desk. His other chair was full of papers and books again.

Jonathan started to get up to give me his chair, but I motioned for him to sit back down. He folded his hands and rested his elbows on the arms of the chair, then gave a deep sigh. "Sounds like you've heard some of the history between me and Kirsten."

I nodded. "Dr. Cannon told me a little. Kirsten told me her version. I walked back to campus with her last night."

Jonathan rolled his eyes. "I can imagine what her version consisted of."

I didn't comment. "I'm just fascinated by the idea that you have, or had, an antidote for the zombie poison."

"Before it disappeared, I had applied for a grant to do research on developing it."

"How would that have been useful?" I asked.

"What do you mean?"

"I mean, if you were able to create an antidote for tetrodotoxin, how would it help the drug industry?"

He took a moment to collect his thoughts. "Because it's a powerful neurotoxin, tetrodotoxin is used in some anesthetic procedures here in the States. It's also a major cause of death and near-death experiences in Japan among those who eat blowfish."

"Fugu, right? It's considered a delicacy over there. Rich people pay for the privilege of taking their lives in their own hands."

He nodded. "Right now, very little can be done for those who succumb to tetrodotoxin poisoning. If we can isolate the active ingredients and make a counteragent for tetrodotoxin, it would open up a whole new area of research. Right now, there are a few companies that are poised to offer antidotes, but none of them reverse the process of shutting down a victim's system. There are still bugs to be worked out."

"But you're an anthropology major, not an ethnobotany major or an authority in chemistry or pharmaceuticals," I pointed out. "How did you come by this antidote?"

"While I was in the Peace Corps in Haiti, I befriended a *bourreau,* the executioner of the local *bizango* society. Jean Toussaint, the *bourreau,* gave me a portion of his powder. We had become very close over the four years I lived there. On the night before I was to leave, Jean and I were sitting around, drinking *clairin,* and he told me he had a farewell present for me." I had read about *clairin.* It was white rum that was often used in voodoo ceremonies. "He knew the zombie poison and the antidote fascinated me, so he presented me with a vial of the powder. He swore me to secrecy."

"There was no list, just the vial?"

He shook his head. "Jean was going against his *houngan* by giving me some of the antidote for study. Most poison makers guard their antidote even more closely than their zombie dust. I just didn't think anyone would try to cut me out of the research. I was so naive.''

"Do you remember any of the ingredients?''

He gave a short laugh and rocked the chair back on two legs, balancing his feet on a pile of papers on his desk. "Yeah, ground human bones, several indigenous herbs, but I know there was more to it—properties that we may have to search the Haitian land for, that may not even be catalogued.''

"Why didn't you get a safe or put it in a safety deposit box?''

"It just didn't seem to me that anyone would, you know, be treacherous enough to steal the formula.''

"And you went to Kirsten because she's an ethnobotanist.''

"Yeah. She was very interested. Then we broke up. And I met Amy around the same time.'' He settled the chair back on all four legs and put his feet back on the floor, then stood up. "Would you like some coffee?''

I shook my head. "Thanks, no.''

He went over to the coffeepot in the corner and poured himself a cup. "Why are you so interested in all of this?''

"Well, I was told some of it by Dr. Cannon, and

I guess I was just curious about filling in the rest." I hoped that would satisfy him. "Did you have a chemist lined up?"

He nodded. "Yeah, one of the professors in the chemistry department, Dr. Thompson, used to work for a big pharmaceutical firm. He was really excited about the impending research. It would have been a big coup—not just for me, but for several other people."

"What makes you think it was Kirsten who took the formula? Why not your chemistry professor?"

"Dr. Thompson never had access to the antidote without me in the room. The night that we broke up, Kirsten came to my apartment to get some of her things. When she left, I discovered that the formula was gone."

"Can't you get more of it from Jean?"

Jonathan smiled, but it was a sad smile. "Jean has vanished. In fact, I thought of that and called the day after I discovered it was missing. Henri, the society priest, told me that Jean had disappeared from the village just a few days before. Henri told me that it was a *djab,* the Haitian equivalent of a demon, who took him away. He mentioned that Jean had done a very bad thing by giving me the formula without consulting the *hounsis* and that he was being punished. I don't know who told Henri and the *bizango* society about Jean's betrayal. It was not for Jean to give to me—it was a decision that should have been made by the entire *hounsis*." *Hounsis* was the word for members of the society.

Hmmm. That was odd. Jean Toussaint vanished from Haiti right before Jonathan's formula disappeared.

"So how is it that you have so much faith in this antidote?"

"Because I saw it work. I have it documented on video."

My ears perked up. "Interesting. Is the video missing as well?"

"I still have it," he said.

"Wow, really? I'd love to see it." He looked at me with suspicion. "In your presence, of course."

He seemed to think about it. "Sure. Are you attending Simon's gallery party tonight?"

I nodded. "Sure."

"How about after the party?"

"Great." My mind was still working on the idea of Jean Toussaint—could he be here in Vermont? Maybe he had second thoughts about giving Jonathan the antidote. Maybe he stole the formula. But that was several months ago. Four, to be exact. He could have left the States by now; he could be back in Haiti, safe and sound. Or maybe the *djab* had taken Jean Toussaint's soul—maybe *he* was a zombie, working on someone's plantation.

And what about Kirsten? If she had taken the formula, maybe she didn't steal the formula to use it, but to keep Jonathan from getting ahead of her in the antidote research game.

And if Amy was a victim of tetrodotoxin poisoning, who and why would anyone give her the poison? And had she escaped by herself, or been helped by the person who poisoned her? Was the poison for her, or for Jonathan? If it was for him, why hadn't he ended up poisoned?

Jonathan looked at his watch and grimaced.

"Something wrong?"

"I meant to go home and get a few books and a paper I left on my desk."

"I'm sorry," I said. "I kept you from working. If there's anything I can do—"

He hesitated, then said, "Well, actually, I do have a couple of things that need to be done this morning, and I won't have time to get them done because I'm filling in for the professor until his meeting ends. These department meetings can last for hours." He rolled his eyes.

"Sure." I tried to inject some enthusiasm into my tone, but I doubted Jonathan could think of anything other than his pressing needs. He was writing some notes on a piece of paper. Then he handed it to me. "I left a few things back at my house. Do you mind picking them up?" He gave me a key. A key! He couldn't have made it easier for me if he'd told me when he'd be gone.

I had enough presence of mind to ask, "Are you sure you trust me? I mean, you told me about the tape and—"

He smiled. "You're very sweet, you know. You put on a tough exterior, but I get the feeling you're not out for yourself." He sighed and looked down. "I think after my experience with Kirsten, I've learned how to read people much better. Amy was good at reading people." He looked up at me and smiled. "She would have liked you."

I returned his smile. "And I think I would have liked her."

"It's her house, you know. She bought it with some of her inheritance. It was a good investment. When we graduated and got married, she said we could either sell it or rent it out to some other grad student."

"I understand there hasn't been any memorial service yet."

Again, he looked sad. "Amy left no one to inherit. No relatives, we hadn't gotten married yet, and her estate has gone to the government to untangle. She was quite wealthy. Not that her money meant anything to me. But I guess I have taken some advantage—I still live in her house. Until some government official knocks on the door and tells me to evacuate the premises.''

I nodded, thinking how hard it must be for him— he wasn't officially a part of Amy's life, and it would get messy when the government stepped in and took possession of the house and Amy's belongings.

And no one had told him that Amy was missing from her drawer in the morgue. I wavered, thinking maybe I should tell him, but remembered I'd be meeting Jack soon, and if he could do a background search on Jonathan, I could lay some of my misgivings to rest. Someone had fed Amy the zombie poison—if, in fact, that was what happened to her—and he had the best opportunity.

''Are you sure you're able to do this errand for me? Do you have any classes that interfere?'' he asked.

I shook my head. ''It won't take that long. My class isn't until this afternoon.''

He nodded, then looked at his watch again and jumped up. ''I have to go teach that class. I'll be back here this afternoon from one to two. Can you bring the books by?''

I nodded. ''I have an early lunch date, so one will be fine.''

''Lunch date, huh?'' He grinned. ''You're a fast mover.''

I shrugged. "Just a guy who takes the ethnobotany course with me. I think we're going to discuss the toxin possibilities for our papers."

He nodded shortly, clearly ready to go. I noted that he wore a long-sleeved shirt and a tie, and a pair of dark slacks. He had dressed up for the occasion of teaching the class.

As we left the office, he straightened from locking the door. "Oh, yes. Did I tell you where I live?"

I hit my head with the heel of my hand in mocking fashion and said, "I forgot to ask." I'd forgotten to ask because I already knew where he lived. Or, I should say, where Amy had lived.

He rattled off the address, then gave me a cell phone number. "In case you miss the one to two o'clock open office time." Then he was gone, half running to get to his class on time.

I couldn't believe my luck—I didn't have to find an open window and risk jail time to look for the zombie poison. Jonathan had given me a key to Amy's house!

I checked the time—I had an hour and a half before I had to meet Jack. My fingers itched where I clasped the metal of Amy's house key, and my stomach fluttered at the thought of meeting Jack later.

TEN

AMY HAD LIVED in a little blue bungalow at the end of a small dead-end street called Carpenter Drive. I marched up the steps and put the key in the door, and it turned easily. Of course it did—it was Jonathan's key.

I stepped into the front hallway, which opened into a large neat front room decorated in upscale student style: cinder-block bookcases filled with books on anthropology and other related subjects, a few bestselling novels, and the occasional primitive figurine or vase. The furniture was a little more substantial—modern couch with foldout futon bed and two flanking fifties easy chairs upholstered in some kind of black nubby material. An entertainment center sat in a corner almost as an afterthought with the requisite big-screen TV, VCR, DVD players, and multiple CD player evident. Two modern wavy black wire CD holders flanked the entertainment center and held over one hundred CDs of Aretha Franklin, the Beatles, the Stones, Bonnie Raitt, and some current groups like Hootie and the Blow-fish (ha!), Matchbox 20, Luscious Jackson, and the Goo Goo Dolls. There was also a section on music native to Haiti.

A small desk was in the opposite corner with an orange iMac and printer sitting on it. Papers were scattered on the top of the desk, and I noticed that the computer was on. I knew quite a few people who left their computers on all the time. I went over and touched the mouse, and the screen popped up. I called up the files, and, from the look of them, this was Jonathan's computer.

I closed the window to leave the computer exactly as I'd found it. There was no reason for me to go snooping in his computer unless I had stronger suspicions. My hand hovered over the mouse, and I decided what the hell.

Most of his files were related to work. One file was for letters. He had his resume at the ready and had applied to several colleges and universities as a professor. There were two letters to someone named Quinlan at Harvard regarding Jonathan's antidote. The last letter was almost heartbreaking, with the concluding lines: ''I regret to inform you that the antidote described in my previous letter has fallen into the hands of someone else.

''If, at some future date, I am able to recover the information, I will be back in touch.''

The letter was signed "Jonathan Sharpe."

I printed out copies of the pertinent information and closed the file, then found the books Jonathan had requested. I put the books and the briefcase with the papers in it by the door. I looked through the videotapes that were neatly stacked on a shelf of the entertainment center, but the tapes were all coded in a way that I couldn't understand. I would have liked the opportunity to watch the tape that was Jonathan's proof that an antidote existed. I'd just have to watch the tape later.

I checked out the other rooms, keeping track of the time so I wouldn't miss lunch with Jack.

The bedroom didn't appear to be lived in. I wondered if both Jonathan and Amy were neatniks or if, after she died, Jonathan became obsessively orderly. I got the impression that Jonathan was living as if each day was the last he would be allowed to stay here.

Looking around, I was struck by how spartan the bedroom looked—a bed and an old chest of drawers. I went carefully through the drawers, and it was clear that Amy and Jonathan shared the chest, half a drawer for him and half for her. The poison clearly couldn't have been sprinkled here without getting some on Jonathan's clothes.

The only bit of personality to the room was the deco vanity that sat in front of the picture window, which was probably there for Amy to catch the natural light in the morning when she made up her face.

I tried to picture where zombie poison could have been scattered that Jonathan wouldn't go, and the only place that came to me was the vanity. The makeup. I opened the round box of finishing powder—it was the loose kind, which would be perfect for mixing in a little zombie dust. I studied the powder in the natural light. Finishing powder tended to be very fine. I tilted the powder one way and the other but couldn't tell.

I took out one of my baggies, slipped on a pair of surgical gloves, and shook a little of it into the baggie, labeling it to make sure I didn't mix up anything. Now I tilted it back and forth to examine it. The light wasn't good, but I thought I saw some unevenly ground powder that didn't have any color. A shiver ran down my spine.

To be thorough, I looked in the bathroom, but I came to the conclusion that it was too communal. Jonathan would have been in contact with any poison that might be scattered on the tile floor, over the counter, wherever. I checked the medicine cabinet, took out the container of medicated powder, and shook some into a baggie, just in case. If I was thorough enough, I would not have to come back.

The kitchen was much the same—too many opportunities for Jonathan to come in contact with the same items as Amy. I still didn't understand why Amy had been the target and Jonathan wasn't touched, but if the poison had been meant for him, he would have come in contact with it by now.

The vanity truly was the only area that he probably never touched. I went back to the vanity and looked it over for anything I might have missed.

The second bedroom was a combination guest room and office. Another futon convertible couch sat against one wall and a very nice state-of-the-art computer setup on a cinderblock-and-door desk. Surprisingly, the computer was still on. Turning it off was probably one of the things he just hadn't gotten around to doing since Amy's death.

I leaned over the computer and clicked on the files. A window popped up, and I clicked on thesis.doc. It was a paper on the identification of victims of the serial killer Kenny Dwayne Green. He was a drifter who killed indiscriminately and traveled the country via railroad. He had been caught in the Houston rail yards and held in jail, but a technical snafu let him out, and he had disappeared from sight.

I read bits and pieces of Amy's thesis, but it was too technical for me to understand. So much for my career as a forensic anthropologist. But my career as a private investigator was alive and well. My mind kept drifting back to Jean Toussaint. And Kirsten. And Simon, the Haitian artist. I needed to talk to him.

I looked at the time. I had ten minutes to meet Jack. I closed the file, grabbed Jonathan's items, and locked the door.

When I arrived, Jack already had his meal and had grabbed a table. I slung my bag on the empty chair. "Watch that for me while I go order?" I asked.

"Sure. I won't start without you." He grinned. I noticed how long his sideburns were, and with the wire-rimmed glasses and shock of dark hair that fell over his forehead, he was definitely a babe.

A young girl with honey-colored hair that fell in natural waves around her smooth shoulders slowed down when she saw Jack. "Hi, Jack. Mind if I join you?" I noticed that she managed to ignore me very nicely, thank you.

He smiled at her. "Thanks for the offer, Leslie, but"—he gestured to me, and she was forced to acknowledge my presence—"I already have a lunch date."

I waved and smiled.

She gave me a flat look and turned to Jack, pouting prettily. "Well, I hope I can take a rain check. I'd like to talk to you about that computer networking class."

I was grateful that neither of them suggested that she join us anyway.

After she moved off, he turned to me. "Sorry about that. Maybe we should have gone off campus for lunch."

I grimaced. "Not enough time. I have to drop off a few things to Jonathan Sharpe, Dr. Cannon's assistant, between one and two."

"Go get your lunch, and then tell me all about it," he suggested.

I walked away thinking about how much his presence was growing on me. I'd only met him the day before, and already I felt comfortable with him. Of course, part of the attraction was that everyone else I was in contact with here at Hartmore was somehow connected to a dead girl. My immediate feeling was that I wanted to confess everything to him—the fact that I was a private investigator, that this was an undercover job, and that I had seen a dead person walking around last night.

Nah, he'd never believe the last one, and I didn't want him to think I was a nutcase. But maybe I could feel him out, so to speak, for confession time later on. I didn't have a whole lot of time to work with.

I did talk about the pizza party.

"Weird." He shook his head. We were down to our drinks at this point.

"What do you know about Kirsten Sorenson-Andersen?"

Jack shrugged. "She's just my teacher. But I've often thought that if she took off the glasses, she'd probably be a babe."

"How long has she been teaching here at Hartmore?"

"She's been here on a grant for the last two terms. She's considered a lecturer here rather than an instructor, and I guess she's completing a paper for the *Journal of Anthropology*. Rumor has it that the National Geographic Society is considering her proposal to fund a research expedition to the Caribbean islands to look for an antidote for tetrodotoxin. You know, the zombie poison."

That was interesting to know. Maybe Kirsten had stolen Jonathan's formula after all, so she could "discover" it later on—after she had gotten a nice fat grant to fund the expedition. I wondered whom she planned to take along on her trip.

"What do you know about Simon Lynch?"

Jack shrugged and picked up the apple that had remained untouched on his lunch plate. He examined it. "He's some hot artist from Haiti, I think. He teaches an art course, and his stuff will be on display in the art gallery tomorrow." He looked at me and winked. "I'm not much of an artist myself. Unless I work with a computer."

We discussed our papers. I talked about doing a paper on tetrodotoxin. He shook his head. "Man, you picked the toughest one to do—Ms. Andersen considers that poison to be her specialty."

My shoulders slumped. Even though I knew I wouldn't be doing a paper, I was still disappointed.

"You seem to be interested in Haiti and the zombie poison," Jack said. "So why don't you do a paper on a related toxin like the zombie's cucumber? It's not as toxic, and really has more of a mythic background than an effect on people."

I nodded. "Okay. What toxin are you writing about?"

He grinned. "The Calabar bean."

Reading up on zombies, I'd seen a mention of it in *Dark Passage*—the Calabar bean was used by tribes along the Niger River in Africa for enforcement of laws by the elders.

"You don't plan to do any subjective experimenting, do you?"

A twinkle in his eye told me he was enjoying the flirting. "I doubt that either of us would find it pleasant."

I laughed. "Yeah, isn't the Calabar bean ground up and given to accused lawbreakers to determine their innocence? I forgot—what are the effects?"

"Paralysis of the spinal cord. The elders make the accused drink a concoction of ground-up beans, then they have to walk a line—sort of like the test for intoxication. Only the accused has to vomit up the mixture before it causes a horrible and painful death.''

"Oooh, lovely," I said.

We were silent for a moment.

"Um, Angela, I was wondering if you'd be interested in taking in a movie tonight.''

I had plans to go to Simon's gallery opening, and later, to break into Kirsten Sorenson-Andersen's house, if I could find it. I knew she would be at the gallery opening, and I had to put in an appearance there, and I definitely wanted to talk to Simon.

I was disappointed. Damn, I had to work. "Tonight would be bad. Dr. Cannon invited me to the gallery opening.''

He raised his eyebrows. "Ah, that's why you asked about Simon.''

I shrugged. "I just don't know much about his work and was wondering about his reputation.''

"Why?" Jack studied me uneasily. "Are you interested in him?''

I laughed. "Not that way. My little sister is an art history major. I'm just curious about him as an artist. I'm wondering if his work will appreciate in value.''

He grinned. "I'm the last person to ask. But you

had me worried there for a minute. I thought you might be interested in the artistic type.''

I suppressed a grin and said, ''Nah, I'm more interested in the computer type.''

He sat up straighter and winked. ''Like I said, computers are my specialty.'' He took a bite of his apple.

I still hadn't had an opportunity to bring up Amy Garrett. I wanted to find out if he knew her. ''Well, I'd better get this stuff to Jonathan. He gave me a key to his house. Actually, it's not officially his house. It belongs to his girlfriend, Amy Garrett.''

''Oh, yeah, Amy.'' We had gotten up and tossed our trash and stashed our trays. ''I was really sorry to hear about her death. Amy and I took a class in computer graphics together. She was really good at her job. And a really nice person.''

''Weird how she just collapsed.''

''Yeah, she was pretty healthy.''

''Did you ever meet Jonathan Sharpe?''

He held the door to the outside for me. Wow, I hadn't been treated with this much courtesy since Reg left. I missed being in a relationship, especially those first few weeks when the excitement and attraction are heightened for both partners.

''I met him briefly at a concert here at Hartmore. Leon Redbone, I think it was.''

"Wow, Leon Redbone was here? I love his music!"

"Me, too. I have most of his CDs," Jack said.

We talked a little about our favorite musicians and discovered that we had similar eclectic taste in music.

A thought occurred to me. "I don't suppose you'd be interested in attending the art opening tonight with me?"

He winked. "It's a date."

We decided on the time and place where we'd meet, and parted to go our ways. I was already looking forward to tonight. But I had to be careful to keep in mind that I was only here for a short time. And Jack had at least six months to go to get his degree. Besides, he was probably way too young for me.

ELEVEN

I STOPPED BY Dr. Cannon's office to drop off Jonathan's things. The door was closed, but ajar, and I thought nothing of knocking quickly, then opening the door.

"Sorry to barge in, but—" I opened the door, and there was Jonathan with Savanna in his arms. I blinked. Savanna gave me the sort of look a cat gives her owner after snagging a chicken leg and consuming it—satisfied and knowing full well what the aftereffects will be. I had no interest in Jonathan romantically—but I don't believe in encroaching on grieving fiancés a week after their loss. I put the briefcase down on the floor and extended the books to him. He disentangled himself from Savanna's octopuslike grip and took the books.

Today, Savanna was wearing a red-and-black plaid miniskirt and a V-necked formfitting sweater. She thrust a hip out and pouted.

"Thanks, Angela. Um, this isn't what it looks like."

Savanna's cat eyes and sly smile told me otherwise.

I shrugged. "Everyone has their own way of grieving," was all I could manage to say. I looked at my watch. "I have an appointment." I was trying to save face after barging in on his tryst.

Jonathan seemed to remember that Savanna was there, and he addressed her. "I think that we've discussed the subject thoroughly." He gathered up the briefcase and selected one of the books, shuttling Savanna out ahead of him. "Wait for me, Angie. I'll walk out with you."

Savanna's sly look changed back to a pout. I was beginning to think that the girl had only two looks. What was it with some college girls and their attempts to snare a man? College apparently hadn't changed much since I had attended ten years ago. There were still girls who spent more time chasing the object of their hormones than working for that degree. It wasn't all that comforting to know that times may change, but human behavior remains the same.

"Umm," I said, flustered, "thanks, but no thanks." I turned around and walked away quickly, not looking back.

"Really, it wasn't what you think, Angela," he repeated as he broke into a trot to keep up with me. He put a hand on my shoulder. I was actually feeling bad for Savanna. I could hear her trying to get his attention as he struggled to catch up to me.

I shrugged sharply to get his hand off my shoulder. "Jon, I'm not your keeper. You can do whatever you want. And I'm certainly not your girlfriend, so you have no obligation to explain yourself." I just wanted to get away. I was embarrassed for him, but he wouldn't leave me alone.

He grabbed my arm and stopped me, spinning me around. His eyes had narrowed, and his jaw was set. "Look, I was stupid for letting Savanna into the office without anyone around. She set her sights on me from the first day she saw me, even though she knew that Amy and I were involved." He paused, looking uncomfortable. "I loved Amy, and we'd talked about getting married. If I could get her back right now, I'd do it in a minute."

I could see the fire and the frustration in his eyes, and God help me, I almost told him what was going on. But I could at least put a few things to think about in his head.

"Jonathan, tell me something—before Amy died, what were her symptoms?"

"She was dizzy and felt cold. And she said she felt tingly all over, especially her hands and feet."

I sighed impatiently. "Doesn't that suggest something to you?"

"No, I—wait a minute, are you suggesting—?"

I shrugged. Well, I was in for a penny, in for a pound. I probably shouldn't have gotten him thinking about Amy being alive. I might have gotten his hopes up for nothing, and all because I was embarrassed about witnessing him and Savanna in a clinch in the doc's office.

A look of horror passed over his face. "My God, she could be buried alive—the mortician could be preparing her for burial—"

I held up a hand. "You told me that the state was looking for heirs. They won't touch her until they schedule an autopsy."

He ran a hand through his hair. "Maybe I should go talk to the police."

I didn't say anything.

"I don't know what to do."

Dr. Cannon walked down the hall toward us. He saw me first and nodded. He stopped walking when he saw the serious look on my face.

"What's happening, Angela?"

I nodded to Jonathan. "I think it's time we tell him what's been going on. I think he'll be more help to us than he is right now."

Cannon fell silent and stroked his beard thoughtfully. Jonathan turned to look at him.

"Let's go into my office and talk, Jon." Jonathan nodded and headed for the office. Cannon stayed behind.

"I'm sorry I didn't wait to talk to you, but I think things are coming to a head," I said. I gave him a quick rundown of what I'd been working on recently.

My client sighed. "Yeah, I told you when you started the investigation that if you thought it was necessary to tell him, do it."

"I gave him something to think about. Now you need to talk to him and tell him what you think he needs to know beyond Amy's apparent death." I told him that I was going to the party tonight, but I needed to get some information first.

I left him to talk to Jonathan, and headed for the Bronco. I had to get away from here for a little while. I needed to call Rosa and see if Antonia had come up with information. I had Jean Toussaint's name to add to the list of background checks.

Near the campus I found a copy center where they had a fax machine, and I got a card with the fax number on it.

I walked a little farther into Bristol and discovered a little diner on the wrong side of the tracks. It was a step back in time, with a soda fountain and a real telephone booth, the kind that doesn't exist much anymore. It afforded me the kind of privacy I needed.

I dialed Rosa's number, and she answered.

"Sarge!"

"Hey, Rosa, were you able to get in touch with Antonia?"

"Gee, Angie, I had to call all over before I found out Antonia is in Europe."

"Europe!" I shouldn't have been surprised—Antonia used to be a model before she turned to computers. We always joked that she was the most beautiful computer nerd in the world.

"Any chance we can reach her?"

"Sarge, she's in Monte Carlo, working for one of the members of the royal family on some kind of computer security system."

This was as close to a disaster as could happen to me. I had come to rely on background checks as part of an investigation of this magnitude. And now I was stuck in this podunk town without access to a computer expert who could do background checks. "Can you think of anyone I can use—anyone with skip-tracing experience?" I asked.

Rosa sounded close to tears. "Gee, Sarge, I've already been asking around and come up empty. I'll keep asking around, but I think I'm gonna have to start looking at the high school level."

That was all I needed—some overeager fifteen-year-old who breaks into the Pentagon files for fun. I had a quick vision of myself in bright orange, holding my prison number up while they took the full front and side views of my head and shoulders.

"That's okay, Rosa. I'll find someone here in Bristol. There's a computer department here at the college. I'm sure I can find someone here." I thanked Rosa and assured her she had done all she could for me, then we hung up.

Skip T had been my computer source for background checks for a few years, but he disappeared. Of course, I'd never really met him. But he'd gone underground and hadn't emerged yet. Antonia had helped me on my last few cases, but she was becoming unreliable due to her work as a computer security consultant. Now I had no one. My mind briefly flirted with the idea of calling Chuck Eddy, but he was such a slime, I couldn't bring myself to do it.

There was the possibility of danger here at Hartmore for whoever got these background checks for me, but I needed someone fast. I thought about the people I knew—Jack was the best possibility. He had mentioned that he was a computer major. He probably knew someone who could do the work, and do it quickly and discreetly. I was going to see Jack tonight, and would have to find a time, and a way, to ask him. It would mean blowing my cover, but I was desperate.

It seemed to me that my entire investigation hinged on getting these background checks. I had a

strong feeling there would be a connection somewhere.

I felt as if something were crawling up my neck:
I looked around—it was as if someone was watching me. I'd felt that way the other day when I went
to Sergeant Zymm as a courtesy call.

I went back to my dorm, feeling drained. I didn't
know Jack's number, but I knew I'd see him tonight. I'd have to find a way to bring up the subject
then.

Savanna was in the room, listening to another
horrid singer. She was working on her computer.

"Hey," I said.

She looked up. "Hey." She seemed less sure of
herself than she had been earlier in Cannon's office
with Jonathan, but she acted as if nothing had happened.

Roxie knocked on the door.

"Hey, Roxie, come on in. Want to help me with
my German lit paper?" Savanna was frowning at
whatever she was writing on the computer.

It was clear I would get no sleep here. I fervently
wished for another night at the glorious bed-and-
breakfast. I collapsed on my bed, hoping they
would get the hint. Apparently Roxie got the hint.

"Hey, Savanna, I was planning on going to the
library. Wanna go with me? We do have that chemistry project to work on."

Savanna wrinkled her nose. "Too much quiet and too many books."

My eyes met Roxie's, and I instantly liked her. "Chemistry, huh?"

"I'm a chem major. We're taking an elective course that involves testing an unknown substance and breaking it down into its most basic elements."

"Sounds interesting," I replied.

Roxie studied me for a moment, then turned to Savanna. "Um, I saw that teaching assistant heading there, the one that you like."

Savanna popped out of her chair and grabbed her book bag. "Let's go." She threw me an enigmatic look— I wasn't sure what to make of it. Jealousy? Anger? Annoyance?

Once she was gone, I drifted off, dreaming of voodoo drums and dolls, Simon Lynch and Kirsten Sorenson-Andersen, and Amy Garrett as a zombie.

THE SLAMMING OF the door startled me awake. Savanna stood over me.

"Some guy is here to see you," she said cheerfully. "And he's kind of hot, if you take his glasses off."

I jumped out of my bed and looked around, wiping the sleep out of my eyes. I ran a brush through my hair and slipped into a printed broomstick skirt and black blouse, the only dressy clothes I'd brought with me. A pair of black flats and an unconstructed black blazer completed my college date look.

Savanna watched me with growing horror. "That's all you're going to do? No makeup? No perfume?"

I shook my head. "Nope. What you see is what you get."

"Where are you going?"

"Dr. Cannon invited me to Simon Lynch's open house at the art gallery."

She looked thoughtful. "Oh. I was invited, but I'm not that interested. I'd go if Jonathan called to invite me," she said in a wistful tone. Suddenly she seemed so young and vulnerable.

I hesitated, then said, "Can I give you a little advice?"

She pouted. "You're not interested in him, are you?"

I gestured toward the door, where Jack waited for me in the hall. "He's the one I'm interested in at the moment. Jonathan is a friend and a colleague. He's also just getting over his girlfriend's tragic death."

"But he kissed me in the office!" She pouted again. It was like dealing with a baby in a woman's body.

I tried to be patient and understanding. "He's

grieving, but he's not dead, Savanna! He told me that you almost forced yourself on him, and he was startled."

"That's not true!" Her voice rose, and she looked angry.

I was about to read Savanna the riot act when a knock at the door broke the tension. "Angela? Are you ready to go?" Jack asked.

I opened the door and smiled. "Yeah. I'm ready. Sorry you had to wait."

He stepped back and looked at me. "You're definitely worth waiting for."

He was worth waiting for as well. Jack had given up his jeans for a pair of khakis and a cool fifties bowling shirt in red, aqua, and black. He wore a black corduroy jacket over the shirt.

We walked across campus to the art gallery, which was located near the chapel and the art department building. I was contemplating the fact that I still had to find the right time to ask him. I had tried to figure out a way to ask about getting background checks without telling him I was a private investigator, but I couldn't figure out how to do it.

"Hey, Angela, are you with me or not?" Jack shook my shoulder lightly.

I came back to the present. "Yeah, sorry. I was taking a little nap when you arrived, and it takes me a few minutes to wake up."

He laughed and put an arm around my shoulders. I felt comfortable and safe with him. I liked his smell—leather and spice.

The gallery was all lit up, and people were streaming in from all different directions. I could tell whether they were faculty, administration, or students by the way they dressed. Administration dressed in suits and sophisticated dresses; faculty members wore nice sweaters or jackets over shirts, or more casual, comfortable dresses; and students who had been invited wore jeans or khakis with nice shirts or tops. Some of the female students wore broomstick skirts like mine.

By the time we got to the entrance, we were holding hands. I hadn't felt this comfortable with someone in a long time.

There was actually someone at the door who took names. He was a student, much too eager with his power, who looked for my name. He shook his head. "I don't see your name on the list." I looked at Jack, and he at me.

"That's okay," Jack said. "We can do something else. There's a Buster Keaton festival at the Student Union."

I needed to get in, and this was an annoyance. And I had to act as if it weren't a big deal.

"That sounds like fun," I said, and I meant it, "but both Simon Lynch and Dr. Cannon asked me, and I know Dr. Cannon needed to speak to me about some research tonight. He told me we'd meet at the party." I paused, and Jack looked totally supportive of my need to get in.

He turned to the party Nazi. "Look, can you just go in there and find Dr. Cannon? Or Simon Lynch?"

The student, who was thin and wore all black, could only be a pretentious art student who thought Warhol was God. He shook his head. "I can't leave the door." God forbid someone who wasn't invited might actually see Simon Lynch's art a day before it was shown to the public. It was like dealing with Cerberus at the gates of Hades.

"Well, if you let me go in there quickly and—" I made a move to walk past him, but he blocked me.

"Look," he said firmly, barring my way, "you're not on the list—" He shook the clipboard at me.

At that moment, Simon came up behind the student and called to me. "Angela! I'm so glad you could make it." He looked over at Jack. "And you brought a friend?"

I introduced them. "I hope you don't mind," I said to Simon. I heard some sort of insistent sound coming from inside.

Simon wore a pair of sun-bleached jeans that

hugged his lean legs and a loose island shirt, something colorful and comfortable looking, which was open to reveal his smooth espresso-colored chest. He had a flat stomach and well-formed shoulders and chest. His lids were at half-mast, and he smelled faintly of marijuana. I wondered how recently he'd smoked a joint. The way he moved was beautiful. "Please. Come on in." He smiled at the Nazi art student. "You don't mind, do you?"

The student shook his head dumbly. As we walked past, I took the clipboard and pen from the student and added my name, then handed it back to him with a smile.

The gallery consisted of stark white walls and bare polished floorboards. Half walls cut the room up, providing more space in which to show work. Simon's works hung on the walls, but I barely had time to glance at them. There was so much to look at, including voodoo flags, religious items that depicted various *loa*, and Haitian gods that hung from the bare rafters. I spied Dr. Cannon talking to Dr. Rathman, who seemed to be with a short stocky woman dressed in an outdated skirt and blouse.

Kirsten was there, looking beautiful in a dark green-print sarong that hugged her curvaceous figure. She had a glass of champagne in her hand, her hair was loose, with an orchid pinned to one side, and she was barefoot. Simon led us up to her. "You know Kirsty."

I could never think of her as Kirsty, only as Kirsten, but it was clear that they were a couple. She moved closer to him as he introduced Jack. The sounds I had heard outside now became clearer—drums, a persistent beat.

"You're the keyboardist with that new band, aren't you?" Kirsten was asking Jack.

Jack nodded. "Yeah, we opened for They Might Be Giants last spring."

"What's your band called again?"

"The Nerds."

Spying someone who had just entered the gallery, Simon excused himself. Kirsten was deep in conversation with Jack, and I slipped away to get glasses of wine for both of us.

I met Dr. Cannon halfway to the refreshment table. He was wearing a pale yellow cardigan over a red-and-brown plaid flannel shirt and brown corduroy slacks.

"I have a theory," I said to him.

"Yes?"

"I think academia keeps the corduroy and khaki manufacturers from going under."

He laughed. "We should buy stock before everyone else figures this theory out." He'd turned around and was walking with me to the refreshment table. I ordered two glasses of red wine, one with an ice cube in it.

"That's unusual," he said.

I shrugged. "Old Italian secret. We're not wine snobs—we refrigerate white *and* red wine." I took a few sips of mine, and when I felt it was cold enough, I discarded the rest of the ice cube. "So tell me, how did it go with Jonathan?"

"He's pretty broken up about it. He won't be coming to this opening."

I nodded.

"But he wanted me to give you this tape, with his apologies. I don't have the faintest idea what he's apologizing for. But he asked that you return it after you've watched it." Dr. Cannon pulled a videotape out of his pocket. I looked around to make sure no one noticed the transaction. I had an inside pocket that was big enough to accommodate the tape.

"Thanks, Doc. By the way, can we talk privately?"

We looked around and found a corner with no one close enough to hear our conversation. I explained about the background checks and Jack.

"I think he'd be the right fellow for the job," Dr. Cannon replied, nodding. "He doesn't have any connection to the department, but he has taken a few anthropology classes."

Dr. Rathman and the woman came up to us, and we had to drop the subject. "Don, I think Angela here has some talent with sculpting. I think forensic anthropology will be a good choice for her in the long run." He patted my shoulder and grinned, and I realized that he was slightly inebriated. I turned to the woman next to him and held out my hand, then realized I had a glass in it. She smiled shyly, and Dr. Cannon took one of my glasses so I could shake her hand and introduce myself.

"Roz Rathman," she said. "Glad to meet you. You take Francis's forensics class?"

We chatted for a few minutes while Dr. Cannon and Dr. Rathman moved away to talk to a couple of other colleagues.

"How long have you lived here?" I asked Roz. She had turned out to be a lively and intelligent woman with a great sense of humor.

"We moved here five years ago. Francis worked for the FBI for ten years, then he went out on his own, contracting to do his specialty to whoever needed his services. We traveled everywhere when he was a consultant."

"Including Haiti?" I asked, gesturing to the voodoo flags and primitive art, which filled the room.

She laughed and nodded. "Yes, we were in Haiti for about a year, working on identification of shipwreck victims."

"That must have been interesting."

She grimaced. "He liked Haiti more than I did. I thought it was dirty and hot and smelly."

I had perked up since learning that the Rathmans had lived in Haiti at one time. "When were you down there? I know there's been a lot of political strife."

"Oh, the politics didn't affect Americans, especially with his work situation. It was almost like there were two countries—one for the Americans and one for the Haitians. But we spent nineteen-ninety-four there, when General Raoul Cedras was in charge." She wrinkled her nose. "He was an awful man. People were taken out of their homes in the middle of the night and were never heard from again. We left about a week after President Aristide came back to run the country. It was really interesting to see the difference just a week made with a democracy in action as opposed to the military regime that was in place for three years." She shuddered.

"Did either you or your husband ever witness any voodoo ceremonies?"

"I didn't," she said. "I don't know about Francis. He would go away for days at a time when he was working. He never expressed any special interest in voodoo around me, though. I'm a wuss about that mystical stuff. I missed attending synagogue while we were there.''

"Angela," Dr. Cannon came up to me, "we'd better rescue your friend Jack. I still have his wine here." He indicated the glass he held in his hand, and I took it from him.

"Thanks." I turned to Roz. "Nice to meet you."

"We'll meet again," she said with a twinkle in her eye.

Cannon and I began to walk back towards Kirsten and Jack. "Look, Doc, I need to get into Kirsten's place. Do you know where she lives?"

He rattled off an address. "It's off-campus housing. She rents an apartment."

"Do you know if she lives by herself?"

He nodded.

"I noticed she's an item with Simon Lynch."

"Yes, but he has his own place to live. He's the resident golden boy right now, and has a studio on campus where he lives and works."

Simon came up to me. "My dear, have you seen my work yet?" He took my arm.

"Oh, am I getting the personal tour?" I asked, glancing at Jack. He had turned away to talk to a tall bearded man who seemed to know him.

Simon acknowledged Dr. Cannon. "I hope you don't mind, Don, if I take her away from you for a time."

Cannon nodded. "I'll let your lovely lady know where you are." I handed the second glass of wine to my client with instructions to deliver it to Jack.

Simon and I started near the entrance. I hadn't studied his collages in depth when I first entered the gallery because I had been so annoyed by the art student/bouncer. The first collage was a mixture of exotic flowers. It was beautiful, but nothing special. Until I looked closer. The flowers formed a face—no, a skull. This one was called *Legba*. The next piece was made up of shells and sand, again forming a symbol of something. I looked at the title, *Damballah Wedo*, and realized that this was Simon's depiction of the serpent god of voodoo. The third collage was entitled *Ayida Wedo*, and was named for the goddess of the rainbow, mate to the serpent god. This one was made up of flowers again, and butterfly wings. It was a rainbow when I first looked at it, then I saw that it was made up of tiny figures.

"These are the children of Damballah and Ayida who reside within her," Simon explained. He moved closer to me. I could feel his heat, and his Haitian accent was lyrical.

"The work is exquisite," I murmured. I felt light-headed and realized I hadn't eaten anything since lunch. There had been food on the refreshment table, but I had Simon alone for now, and I needed to find out so much about him. "Did you create these collages while you were living in Haiti?"

"Yes. I did these back home. I haven't had much time to create anything here in Hartmore while teaching students."

"Where did you study?"

He laughed. "I didn't. I am what the wealthy patrons call a folk artist."

I didn't believe that for a minute. He had studied at a university, I was certain of that. He couldn't be teaching at college level otherwise. But he wanted to preserve some fiction that he was a folk artist, and I had no reason to challenge him on that. "But the work you do is so skilled. Tell me, are all your works voodoo themed?"

He opened his arms to gesture around the room. "Voodoo is a part of Haitian culture that cannot be ignored."

"Where in Haiti did you grow up?"

"A small village called San Poel."

I nodded. "I'm afraid I'm not as well-informed as Kirsten, Jonathan, or Dr. Cannon, so could you tell me how widespread voodoo is in Haiti?"

He smiled, and it nearly devastated me. I felt as if I was caught up in the vortex of Simon's sexual magnetism. He knew he was devastatingly attractive, and he wielded his attractiveness like a weapon. I wondered if anyone really knew him.

"It is the root of my work. It is my life. I grew up a practicing *hounsis* and believing in the *loa,* who guard and protect mankind."

He moved closer to me, and I began to sweat. I glanced around and saw Jack and Kirsten looking over at us. Jack was frowning, and Kirsten's expression was one of impatience.

I forced myself to take a step back from him and turn around to look at another one of his works. This one was scary. It was made of small bits of bones and sticks and stones, and as I looked at it closer, I realized it was the image of a woman— not a spirit, but a zombie. The drums seemed to become louder. I must have said the word *zombie* out loud.

"Yes, that is a zombie." I heard the words close to my ear. I could feel his breath on my neck, and the other sounds—the murmurs of the other people, the Haitian music—all became a buzz in the background. "Do you want to know how I came to create this work?" His voice was low, mesmerizing, intimate. His breath was warm in my ear like a summer night on a Caribbean beach.

"Yes."

"She was my wife back in Haiti. She was the mother of my children. Her name was Françoise, and she was unfaithful to me. So I called for a secret tribunal, and it was agreed that her soul would be taken from her.''

My heart was pounding, and I wanted to move, to break the spell, but I couldn't.

''It is what Haitians fear the most—to have their souls stolen from them. It is the most precious thing we can own, the soul.''

It was as if Simon was wrapped around me in a protective cocoon, and I couldn't break free.

''What happened to her?'' I managed to ask.

''She is working now on a plantation outside of Port-au-Prince.''

''What about her lover?''

''Her lover? What do I care of him?'' His voice became low, and he seemed to surround me. ''You intrigue me, Angela Matelli.'' His voice, his words, thrilled me at the same time that they chilled me. He brushed a strand of hair away from my shoulder, and I shuddered with desire. ''You are not what you appear to be, are you?''

I wanted to answer him, to tell him the truth. What was it with him and Kirsten, I thought laconically. Why did they both see through me? Weariness overtook me. My eyelids drooped. I should have been full of energy after my nap, but not having eaten probably had something to do with it.

Unless Simon had put something in my drink. He could do anything he wanted to me at this point.

The Haitian drums kept beating, but they soon turned into a buzz, faint at first, then louder and louder until it enveloped me. I swayed like a plant in a gentle breeze.

Someone was shaking my arm. And kept shaking my arm. "Angela? Angie? Are you okay?"

I blinked and took a deep breath—it was as if I had been drowning. Simon was gone, and Jack stood before me. I shook my head and ran a hand over my face. I looked around and saw Simon on the opposite side of the room, his back to me.

"Jack." I moved closer to him. I could fight tangible enemies, but I felt vulnerable now. I hadn't been able to ward off Simon. He had the ability to manipulate others and had stripped me of my will with little more than words and the elusive power that he had at his disposal. I wasn't sure whether he was evil incarnate or simply a man with incredible magnetism.

"You're shivering." Jack drew closer.

I felt Jack's body close to mine. I'm not much on things I can't see, but I could feel Jack's presence—he was real, substantial; he had no agenda or evil about him. I didn't feel that way around Simon. I made a vow then and there to never be alone with Simon again. "Let's get out of here." I took Jack's hand, and smiled up at him.

He smiled back, and I felt as if I had communicated my very soul to him without using any words.

TWELVE

I WOKE UP TO sunlight streaming in on my face. My head ached, and I realized that I'd missed an opportunity to break into Kirsten's apartment to search it. I bolted upright in bed and said, "Shit!"

"Good morning to you, too."

Then I looked over to my left. Jack. He was awake and smiling. His smooth chest was bare, and a sheet covered up the rest of him. God, he was good-looking. He had a little shadow on his face, no glasses, and his hair was tousled. I melted.

Then he burst out laughing. "The look on your face when you realized that you weren't alone—"

I reached for my pillow and hit him. He grabbed his pillow and fought back. My headache cleared up, and I yelped as Jack lunged for me, his arms and legs tangling with mine. We lost all interest in our pillow fight. He kissed me and soon we were groping each other, and our sighs mingled and became moans of pleasure.

Much later, we lay side by side like little children. I felt guilty for taking time off to have a relationship. Jeez, I was here in Vermont for a few days, and I had ended up in bed with this gorgeous computer wiz/musician. In the middle of an investigation that involved zombies. Yeesh.

Jack propped himself up on his elbow and looked down at me. I had my hand over my eyes, but I could see his face through the fingers of my hand.

"Are you having second thoughts about us?" Jack asked.

I took my hand away from my face and looked straight at him. "God, no. You saved my life last night. I could never have second thoughts about what we've had." I slid to the edge of the bed and sighed. "But you see," I stopped, not sure how to explain, "I was supposed to do something last night. I had a proposition for you last night."

Jack tried to hold back a smile, and I found my pillow and threw it at him again. "Not that proposition," I said. "A different kind."

My back was to him, but I heard Jack get out of bed and start to dress. I looked around and found bits and pieces of my clothes. I reached for my blouse and skirt, but couldn't find my bra or panties.

As I pulled on my clothes, I looked around. Jack lived in an apartment building off campus. It was a typical bachelor's pad with no sense of decorating. The bedroom consisted of a functional-enough bed, a chest of drawers, and a desk with a state-of-the-art computer on it. I found my blazer in a corner of his room, and as I slipped it back on, I felt the videotape in my inside pocket.

Jack came around the bed and knelt in front of me. "Angela, I know we haven't known each other long, but I felt an immediate attraction to you, and I hope that you feel the same. Maybe we can talk about this proposition over breakfast?"

I smiled and cupped the side of his face with my hand. "I do feel the same way, Jack. It's just that, well, I'm here under false pretenses." I hesitated. "How much do you know about the people I'm working with: Kirsten Sorenson-Andersen, Simon Lynch, Jonathan Sharpe, Dr. Cannon, and Amy Garrett?"

He frowned slightly, then looked up at me. "Not much. Just the fact that I'm taking a class from Ms. Sorenson-Andersen and that Simon Lynch is a talented folk artist, but he's a little too edgy for my taste."

I took stock of my situation and realized that I needed someone up here. I was wishing I'd taken Rosa up on her offer to come with me, but it would have taken more planning than we had time to do. I had to trust someone besides my client. I wasn't sure it had been right to confide in Jonathan since I was undercover, but he was grieving for Amy.

Right now, I needed to talk to someone more than anything else—someone who wasn't my client, someone I could confide in. Rosa wasn't here. Jack would do fine. But I wondered how he would react when I told him about the zombie stuff.

I began to tell him why I was here, and gave him as much information as I felt comfortable with. I told him I'd been hired to look into some weird practical jokes, and that it somehow tied in with a missing antidote for tetrodotoxin. I was relieved when he listened patiently and didn't give me any weird looks.

"So you're a private investigator. I thought all PIs resided in the pages of books by Hammett, Spillane, and Parker. You're much prettier than their private eyes."

I blushed. "I thought you'd be reaching for the phone to call the local Bellevue and inform 'em one of their residents had escaped."

Jack grinned, then leaned over and kissed me. "You forget—I saw how Simon had you—forgive me—spellbound last night. I think it was the most amazing and frightening thing I've ever seen."

I held up a finger to make my point. "That can be explained. I hadn't eaten anything since lunch."

He laughed. "Well, don't make that mistake

again. And as for zombies, need I remind you that I'm taking the ethnobotany course? I've read ahead on tetrodotoxin. And I did take a course from Dr. Cannon last term. I know it happens.''

''Not in Vermont it doesn't.''

He tilted his head and kissed me again. ''Let me help you.''

''You've helped just by letting me talk to you. What I've missed since I've been up here is someone to talk to.'' I paused, then added, ''But your help on background checks for my list of suspects would be mightily appreciated. I can pay you.''

He shook his head. ''I'll do it because we're— you're my...'' He trailed off and turned red.

''You'll do it because I will put you on my expense account,'' I said. ''My client has already agreed to it. Besides, I want to keep my private life and professional life separate.''

''Well, I could use the money for living expenses,'' he said sheepishly. Then he brightened. ''Breakfast?''

I nodded, my stomach already rumbling in anticipation. My hand brushed the tape again. ''Before we eat, do you have a VCR?''

He nodded and led me into the living room. As I walked through the place, I got the impression that he had at least one roommate, and the stark bachelor look of his bedroom extended to the rest of the place. The only two rooms that looked lived-in were the bathroom, where dirty wet towels decorated the towel racks and an almost empty bottle of antibacterial hand soap seemed to serve no function, and the kitchen, with a counter covered with pizza cartons, open bread bags, and a jar of peanut butter. A slightly rank smell emanated from the sink.

"My roommate practically lives with his girlfriend," he explained. "Dave comes back here to eat occasionally," he gestured to the kitchen, "and to throw the occasional party. It's kind of nice to have the place mostly to myself. I get a lot of studying done." I studied him—he had a five o'clock shadow, and with the sideburns, the wire-rimmed glasses, and his mop of blondish brown hair, he looked like an alternative rocker. I usually didn't go for guys who looked like Jack—my taste ran to preppies and yuppies. I didn't know much about his own background, but there was something about him that made me trust him implicitly.

We slid the tape into the deck and turned on the television. The scene before me was of a Haitian woman, thin to the point of emaciation, seated in a chair in what appeared to be a primitive hospital or clinic. Jonathan came into the shot.

"Tuesday, July second, nineteen-ninety-seven. Today we are here with patient number one. We will call her Isabel. She died nine years ago, and only recently was discovered by a family member when a group of laborers were being driven through their village near Gonaïves. The birthmark on her neck"—here, Jonathan reached over and moved the woman's head to the side—"identified her to family members." Isabel was as docile as a lamb. The camera focused in on a dark mark shaped like Italy, then went back to Isabel. Jonathan was out of the picture again, but his voice came through clearly. "Jean will give her the antidote, and we'll check back later."

The next segment was recorded a week later. Isabel showed signs of life. She was able to respond more spontaneously to questions that she was asked.

This was repeated several more times until Isabel was responding normally and the camera was told that her vital signs had been documented as normal.

Jonathan had documented several more cases, and I fast-forwarded through them, stopping here and there to listen to some narration. If I were to believe the tape, the antidote was truly a miraculous drug that transformed zombified victims back into normal human beings. Clearly Jonathan and Jean Toussaint had taped this in secret.

"Wow," Jack said in a sober tone, "this is bigger than just a few practical jokes, isn't it?"

I shrugged. "I don't know. It depends on whether or not you believe what Jonathan wants us to believe on this tape."

"You mean you're still skeptical?"

"I'm paid to be cynical, to think through all the possibilities." I shrugged. "He could easily have faked the recoveries. I don't know these victims. Do you?"

He seemed to think about it, then nodded. "Maybe you're right. I can do some checking on these cases for you if you'd like. I'm already interested."

Reluctantly, I nodded. "That'd be great. But the background checks are a priority." I gave him a list of my suspects: Kirsten Sorenson-Andersen, Jonathan Sharpe, Simon Lynch, Jean Toussaint, Francis Rathman. I added Amy Garrett and a note for Jack to cross-check Jean Toussaint against every flight from Haiti into the States over the last month. And flights back.

"Let's grab something to eat. Your treat—a business breakfast."

I laughed.

To my relief, Jack suggested we go to the Wild Onion for breakfast. As we walked out, I looked at the address of the apartment building and realized that he lived in the same place as Kirsten Sorenson-Andersen. I tucked that information away. I needed to find the time to get into her place and look around for the antidote.

Breakfast with Jack was more comfortable than I'd expected. I always disliked the day after spending the first night together, and I expected us to be awkward.

I had a pumpkin-pecan muffin and two grande lattes while Jack worked on a bagel. "When do you need the reports?"

"Huh?" Sometimes I amaze myself with the insight I can bring to one utterance. Jack smiled as I sipped my coffee. "Oh, the reports." I looked around to make sure no one could hear us. "Um, as soon as possible. Can you get some of it done today?"

He thought about it. "I'll skip my class today."

"Oh, don't—"

He held up his hand. "Don't worry. I'm ahead on the material."

I squeezed his hand and kissed his cheek. "Thanks, Jack."

We parted with another kiss and a promise to meet back at my dorm room later this afternoon.

I headed back to my dorm. Savanna, thankfully, wasn't there. But her music was playing. She had a 4-CD player, and Fiona Apple was singing. If there's any female singer I hate more than Alanis and Tori, it's Fiona. I went over to her side of the room and turned off the pretentious prattling.

I walked back over to my side of the room and noticed a black object on the bed. On closer inspection, it was a black feather, possibly from a crow. Probably not a good thing. It was a warning. Someone suspected that I wasn't a student. Not a big surprise to me, but it meant I had to be more careful. Yeah, right.

After I showered and changed into clean clothes, I walked over to my client's office. Dr. Cannon wasn't there, but I checked his office schedule. He was supposed to be teaching a class but would be back in the office in an hour and a half.

There wasn't enough time to go anywhere, but I did have time to go over to Kirsten's office, which I'd discovered was down the hall from Cannon's office. Her door was locked, but her schedule was on the door. She was, in fact, teaching a class right now, and I was free. Well, I actually had a class, but I had to keep in mind that I wasn't really a student, and that I shouldn't become worried about working on papers and studying for midterms. I hoped that the investigation would come to a conclusion before I had to turn in papers or take exams.

Okay, it was time for me to get into Kirsten's apartment and see what there was to see. But first,

I needed to go back to my room and get my lock pick set.

Back in the room, Savanna still hadn't come back. Her side of the room looked the same as it had a few hours ago. Roxie knocked on the door. She was wearing another interesting combination of blue and pink with her hair up in two high braids.

"Hey," I said, casually stuffing my lock picks in my purse.

"Has Savanna come back here yet?" she asked.

I shook my head. "I don't think so."

"She wasn't in her lit class." Roxie frowned. "I had a paper I was working on for my psychology class. She was supposed to meet me at the Student Union so we could work on our chemistry project. She told me she had an interesting and mysterious substance for us to work with."

"Savanna doesn't strike me as the most reliable person," I replied as gently as possible. Interesting and mysterious substance? I filed that away in my mind for future reference.

Roxie nodded reluctantly. "It seems that way, but she's pretty serious about the lit class."

"I'll leave a message on the door for her, okay?"

She smiled and thanked me before she left.

As I was locking the door and pinning the message for Savanna on the door, Jack came up the hall. He had a file filled with papers in his hand.

I met him halfway, and he handed me the files. "This is what I've been able to come up with so far."

I scanned the documents I had in my hand and muttered, "Wow," under my breath. I looked up. "I didn't know you could get so much information in such a short amount of time. Thanks for getting this for me." He had information about Kirsten Sorenson-Andersen, Francis Rathman, and Jonathan Sharpe.

"How soon can you get me the information on Lynch and Toussaint?"

"Give me the rest of the day. We'll meet later today, when we agreed? Getting the cross-checking done takes a little more time than this straight background check. What will you be doing until then?"

I winced. "Trust me, Jack, you don't want to know.'

THIRTEEN

I PARKED THE CAR around back of the apartment complex and came in through the alley. The back door had a spring lock, and Jack had told me that he thought Kirsten's apartment was on the second floor. It was an unsecured building, so I went to the front and checked the labels until I found "K. Sorenson-Andersen, 217."

I took the stairs, figuring that I was less likely to run into anyone on the stairs than in the elevator. I knocked on the door and waited to see if anyone would answer. It was like being in a ghost town—no one was around. I could probably yell in the hallways, pound on doors, and generally act like a lunatic, and no one would notice because everyone was at the college either taking classes, reading in the library, or meeting with an instructor about an upcoming term paper or change in majors.

Getting into Kirsten's apartment took more time than I'd expected—she had a bolt lock. It took longer than a spring lock but less time than a dead bolt. Once inside her place, I was cautious, afraid that some half-asleep roomie would stumble out into the living room, but there was no one here.

The living room was furnished with uncomfortable-looking Danish modern furniture, mostly blond wood and pale colors. The comfort factor was low. The place smelled like cigarette smoke. Ashtrays littered the living room. The sofa and matching chairs had an emaciated look, as if upholstered by Ebenezer Scrooge himself trying to save money on foam padding and upholstery fabric. The furniture was designed to keep a visitor from staying too long, as if the room were a fast food restaurant. There was a minimum of family photos—one of an older man and woman, clearly her parents. The man wore a short-sleeved black shirt and slacks and carried a Bible. The woman wore a plain floral-print dress. They both wore pained smiles against a backdrop of huts. A few black children played in the background as well. Another photo showed a younger Kirsten with a much younger girl, also blond, tanned, slender. The younger girl must have been the half sister she had mentioned. The girl looked familiar, but I couldn't place her. She looked so much like Kirsten that I assumed that I was just seeing a carbon copy.

There was no television, but she did have a CD player. Her CDs were mostly in two categories:

Grieg and Caribbean music. Her books were all nonfiction, all related to her work. Her computer was on, and I touched the mouse to get rid of the screensaver.

Once I pulled up the window, I looked through file names: ethno.wp, toxin.wp, anti.wp—

Hmmm. I opened anti.wp and found information documenting various "antidotes" for the zombie poison, but nothing that appeared to be Jonathan's antidote.

I went through the rest of her apartment, wondering if I'd find Amy sitting in a closet or in a corner of the bathroom in her current catatonic state, but no one was sharing Kirsten's apartment as a roomie or as a zombie slave.

When my curiosity was satisfied, I left, taking care to slip out the back way. On my way back to the Bronco, I thought about the other possibilities. There was Simon Lynch and—I couldn't think of anyone else who might have a stake in the antidote. There were the Rathmans, and Jonathan himself. Maybe this was all an elaborate deception of his to assign blame elsewhere for Amy's death.

I went back to Dr. Cannon's office and found Jonathan there.

"Angela. Have you seen Dr. Cannon today?"

I shook my head. "What's up?"

"He had a class this morning. He never misses

class without telling me. It's a good thing I decided to drop by." How convenient, I thought. I hoped Dr. Cannon was just detained somewhere.

This wasn't good. Cannon would have let me know if he was going to do something different from his schedule. I was alarmed by his disappearance.

I took the tape out of my purse and handed it to Jonathan. "By the way, thanks for loaning me the tape. It was fascinating, and I'm honored that you trusted me with it."

Jonathan looked away for a moment, then said, "Well, you're trying to help Dr. Cannon with these anonymous warnings. And you've given me hope that Amy may not be dead." He looked back at me. If he was lying, he was good at it. "I was contacted by the police the other night about Amy. They told me her body was missing and they're looking into it. They suspect it was some prank—maybe some students here at school."

"But where would they put a body?" I asked.

He shrugged. "Like I said, it was just a theory of theirs." He looked at his watch. "Dr. Cannon has another class in a few minutes." He stood up, then said, "How's the investigation going?"

I knew what he was fishing for—whether or not I had found his antidote. I decided the less he knew, the better. I already regretted having opened up to him. "Not great."

"Would you do me a favor and go over to Dr. Cannon's place to see if he's all right?" Jonathan handed me a key. "He may be lying somewhere, hurt."

"Why didn't you go over there earlier?" I asked, suddenly alarmed. Until Jonathan mentioned it, I hadn't thought about Cannon lying in his house, helpless. Maybe I needed another cup of coffee. I took the key from him.

"I called, and no one answered. I thought maybe he'd show up late for class."

I looked at the key, then up at him.

He seemed to understand my unspoken question. "I got that key from his desk. Dr. Cannon showed me where it was in case I needed to get into his house."

I nodded. Savanna suddenly came to mind. "Do you know anything about where Savanna may be?"

Jonathan looked offended. "Why would I know?"

I gave him a look that told him I wasn't buying the innocent act.

"Look, Angela, the only person I should be defending myself to is Amy. I told you before that Savanna was the aggressor. I had no intention of getting involved with another woman so soon after my girlfriend died.''

So he'd thought about it? Amy had been gone for less than a week. Well, Jonathan wasn't dead, and until the other day, he thought his girlfriend was.

''Okay,'' I said, holding my hands up in surrender, ''I believe you.''

I thanked Jonathan and left.

I drove to Cannon's house. I had the key to his house in my jeans pocket. I parked up the street from his house and walked to his place. The street was quiet—everyone was at the college working. Before leaving the car, I took a pair of surgical gloves and several self-closing plastic baggies out of a box that I kept in the back for such occasions.

As I walked up to the door, I noticed that my client's car was not in his driveway. The garage door was closed, but the garage windows were too high for me to peek through. I'd have to go in through the kitchen and check to see if the car was in the garage.

When I walked in, the house smelled funny—the kind of smell that takes over a place when the resident isn't there. I remembered that when I arrived on Sunday night, my client had met me at the front door in his bare feet. I took off my boots and left them by the door. But I left my socks on.

I slipped the gloves on and began to check the places where powder might be strewn. I got the impression that Cannon rarely wore slippers, and, in fact, when I searched for slippers of some sort, I found a pair way back in the far corner of his bedroom closet. I went through every pair of shoes and socks that he owned, hunting for something that looked suspicious.

I found an abandoned frozen dinner by the sink in the kitchen. Opening the door to the garage, I noticed it was empty. Cannon's car was gone.

I checked the trash cans and the rugs of the office, the bathroom and the living room. The answering machine yielded no messages. I went out to his backyard—he had a small garden—and I looked around the yard for signs of a powdery substance on the patio. I was beginning to think that my client had left over some emergency.

I went back through the house and went through a scenario: my client comes home after a hard day in the ivory tower. He takes off his shoes. He takes off his socks and—puts them in the laundry. I went into his laundry room. The floor didn't indicate anything white and powdery, but I began sorting through his laundry basket.

I found several pairs of socks, all with white powdery marks that smelled like medicated talcum powder. I'd found a container of foot powder in his bathroom earlier that smelled just like what was on his socks, but I put them in separate bags and marked them anyway.

Cannon's bedroom was the last place I looked, mainly because it was located in the back of the house at the end of the hall. I had searched the house in an orderly way, starting with the living room, then moving to the dining room, the office, and the bathroom.

The floor was bare polished wood with throw rugs on each side of the king-sized bed. The bed wasn't made, so he had, most likely, slept here last night.

Dr. Cannon kept photos of his family—I assumed they were of his family—that included an elderly couple in front of an RV, a woman around his own age, and a high school graduation picture of a boy and a recent picture of a young girl, grinning, on a swing set. The boy and the girl might be nephew and niece, the woman his sister, and the elderly couple his parents. I carefully searched the chest of drawers and the nearest nightstand. I was walking around the other side of the bed to get to the other nightstand when I realized I'd stepped in something. I looked down and let out a scream. Powder. On the bottom of my sock.

I hobbled to the bathroom and carefully took off my sock. Good thing I was wearing thick cotton socks if this was zombie dust. I rinsed my foot off for good measure. I sniffed the powder-encrusted sock, careful not to inhale it or get it on my skin. It didn't have that medicated smell. It could be my foot odor, but there was some other odor there, a musty graveyard smell.

I went back in the bedroom and studied the powder. It had been disturbed, once by me and possibly earlier by—Dr. Cannon? Still, I could see that the powder had been poured out in a pattern, a symbol of some sort. I'd seen that symbol before—in Simon's art. Could he be involved somehow? I'd always thought it was a possibility.

I looked around the room more carefully, trying to picture what had happened. Cannon would have come into the bedroom last night and gotten ready for bed. He would have gone into the bathroom, and when he came back out, he would have gotten into bed on the side with the powder. He would have been barefoot. Would he have known that the powder was there? Most people turn the lights down in the bedroom before getting ready to sleep. Maybe he'd have had one small light on—the one on the nightstand near the bathroom. Would there have been enough illumination for him to notice the powder? How many people look down at their feet, or at the floor, when they go through a nightly ritual?

I looked around the bathroom more carefully, now that I suspected foul play. His toiletries were still there. In the bedroom, I found his watch and a ring I had seen on him earlier. His wallet was missing, as were the keys to his car. I went back to the office and found his address book. In the front were names and phone numbers of important people. I copied down several of them, including the number of Anita Cannon Bidwell, who was clearly his sister.

Only then did I call Sergeant Zymm. He came to the house within fifteen minutes, accompanied by two uniformed officers.

He didn't look happy. I explained the situation— how I came to be in Dr. Cannon's house, what I suspected might have happened.

One of the officers took pictures of the powder, while the other put on a surgical glove, took out a baggie, and scooped a little of the powder into the baggie.

"Look, Ms. Matelli, this probably isn't what you think it is," Zymm said. "Maybe there was some emergency—a friend ended up in the hospital or something—and he left last night without making arrangements."

"Then why didn't he get in touch with someone this morning? What about the fact that his bags haven't been packed?"

"His car is gone, isn't it?" Zymm pointed out. "Maybe he had more than one set of bags. You don't know if any clothes are missing?"

"His toothbrush and toothpaste are still here. Comb, brush, his watch, and ring—"

Zymm held up his hand. "Ms. Matelli, his wallet is gone. So are his car keys."

He took my elbow and steered me into the living room. "Ms. Matelli, I understand that you came here to make sure everything was all right. In fact, you came here at the urging of Dr. Cannon's teaching assistant."

"Jonathan Sharpe."

He nodded, but his face told me he was gonna have to deliver bad news. "Yeah. And I understand that you entered here under the best of intentions. But Dr. Cannon's a grown man, and until he's been missing forty-eight hours, and a relative, or even an employer, calls in that he's missing, I can't do anything. There's nothing here that says to me, 'Foul play.'" He indicated the powder on the bare wood floor. "It's probably just foot powder."

"But he's had threats before that you've documented."

Zymm gestured for me to settle down, which just succeeded in pissing me off. "Ayeah, but none of those warnings came to anything, did they? This is probably just another one."

"What about Amy Garrett?"

"The body that's missing from the morgue?" Zymm shrugged. "We've interviewed people at the hospital, and no one saw anything."

"No one?" I asked. I couldn't believe that.

"Well, one orderly says he thinks he saw someone, a man most likely, wheeling a gurney out of the hospital around eight on Thursday night." He patted me on the shoulder and handed me my purse. "It sounds like a sick prank, the sort of thing frat houses pull during initiation week. In fact, we're talking to the frat houses, and we'll find the culprit."

I sighed. Zymm clearly had his ideas of how this case was shaping up. He saw the separate pieces and didn't see the whole of it because it was difficult to believe in the voodoo part. I knew I wouldn't be able to convince him otherwise until he had the powder tested.

"You'll let me know if you find Amy?" I asked.

He nodded. "I'll let you know if and when I find the body." Zymm opened the front door. I was pretty sure it was a hint for me to leave.

Still, I turned around and faced Zymm again. "You know this powder is going to contain tetrodotoxin."

He smiled the type of smile that told me he was losing patience with me. "Now, really, Ms. Matelli, where would someone get an exotic poison like that here in Vermont?''

He helped me out the door, and closed it. I stood on the front steps of my client's home and wondered about that: would someone get tetrodotoxin here in Hartmore College?

FOURTEEN

I WENT BACK to my dorm room. Roxie was waiting outside, and she looked worried.

"Savanna's not back yet?"

She shook her head. "Now I *am* worried. I called her folks because I thought that maybe she had gone home for some emergency. I think I worried her mother."

"Why are you going to so much trouble for her?" I asked.

"She's my lab partner for this chemistry class, and we had plans to work on our project today," she said, a bit defensive.

"She doesn't strike me as the most stable partner a girl could choose," I said, trying to be sensitive, but utterly failing.

Roxie smiled. "Ah, but you see, she has to keep her grades up, or her folks will pull the plug on her education. She's more motivated than you probably think."

I made a decision. "Come on. We're going to

check Savanna's things." Before we went into the room, I warned her to keep her shoes on, and I handed her a pair of surgical gloves. "Any powdery substance you find, don't sniff it or inhale it. Don't touch it with your bare hands."

Roxie's eyes got wide. "What's going on here?"

I shrugged. "I don't know, but I think it involves tetrodotoxin, the zombie poison."

She rolled her eyes. "Get out of here. You're paranoid."

It was time to start telling people who I was and why I was here. I hadn't been crazy about the undercover thing in the first place, and now that Dr. Cannon seemed to have disappeared, I had to make a decision.

I grabbed Roxie by her shoulders. "Look, you can help, or you can leave. I'm a private investigator, hired by someone who has since disappeared, and now Savanna is gone as well."

Roxie took only a moment to decide. When she did, she nodded decisively and followed me into the dorm room. While we searched, I thought about how someone would get a body out of this room, out of this building. At night, there would be students moving through the halls at all hours. Even in the middle of the day, there were students here studying or sleeping or goofing off and watching their favorite soap operas in the common room downstairs off the entryway.

Nothing was missing from the room. I found no powder. She had to have gone willingly—someone had called her or had come by and asked her to go with him or her.

The only thing Savanna and I had in common was Anthropology 101, and the only people whom we were jointly acquainted with were Dr. Cannon and Jonathan. Could either man have come by and asked her to go with him for some reason? Roxie had mentioned that Savanna had a mysterious substance for them to test—could it be tetrodotoxin or the antidote?

Roxie went over to the computer. "Let me check to see if she was working on our project for chemistry."

I nodded absently and got up. Outside in the hall, I began knocking on doors. No one answered until I got to the end of the hall. A girl with tousled hair and sleepy red eyes opened the door. She stared grumpily at me.

"Hi, I'm sorry to wake you, but I live down the hall in one-thirty-three. With Savanna."

The girl yawned. "Yeah, I know who she is. What about her?"

"Did you happen to see her go out at any time last night or this morning?"

She shook her head. "Look, you woke me after an all-nighter. Don't expect me to help you find your roommate." She started to close the door. "I was woken up several times this morning, including when the carpeters came by and picked up the old carpeting."

I put my hand on the door to keep her from shutting it. "What did you say? About the carpeting?"

"Some idiot dragged the carpeting outside last night. The janitor pounded on my door this morning and asked me if I'd seen anyone take the carpeting out last night." She rested her forehead against the door, clearly wanting to go back to sleep. "I asked for a single room, and this is my penance—the gatekeeper to the dorm rooms."

I thanked her, and she went back into her room to try to get more sleep. I went into the common room—the new carpeting hadn't been laid down yet. But the old carpeting was gone. I inspected the new carpet—it wasn't terribly big, so probably one fit person could handle it.

I called the maintenance office from the phone in the common room—only calls within the college could be made.

"Yeah," said a harried male voice. "Sam here."

I explained my interest in the old carpet.

"I was the one who went over there to take away

the old carpet. Someone had dragged it outside and left it on the lawn next to the pickup area.''

"Where's that?"

"Go out the front doors and take a left, then take another left."

"What did you do with the carpet?"

"Took it to the dump."

"Was there anything odd about it?'' I asked.

Sam sounded rushed when he answered. "Is there a point to these questions? I dunno. It looked like a rug. There were no bloodstains on it, if that's what you're getting at."

I thanked him and hung up. I walked around the building and found the area where the carpet must have been—it was a small loading dock for moving in and out of the dorm. I'd parked my car here when I moved my bags in the other day. I wondered why anyone would drag a carpet out here, and the one answer that stood out was that there must have been a body concealed in it until the body could be put in a car or truck.

I went back to my room. Roxie was still there, and Jack had joined her. He lit up when I came into the room—at least I like to think that's what he did. "I have the rest of the information you needed." He handed me a file. "You were right about Toussaint. He came into the States about two weeks ago, but he hasn't left yet."

"Thanks." We kissed.

Roxie looked at the file. "What's that?"

I didn't want to get her any more involved than she already was. Whoever had taken Savanna and Dr. Cannon was trying to cover up his or her tracks. I wasn't sure how Savanna fit into the picture, but maybe she discovered something, or maybe someone came to our room looking for me and found her instead.

"Roxie, thanks for your help. How's your schedule?"

She looked at her watch and blinked. "Oh! I've got a philosophy class in ten minutes, and I left my books in my room." She looked up, guilt evident on her face—she had already forgotten the file.

"Go ahead. I've got everything under control," I told her, then glanced at Jack. "We'll take care of everything."

She nodded, but still looked upset. "Do you think that's why she's missing? She told me last night on the phone that she had a powder, something that would pose a challenge for us."

My mind began to turn over the new information. "Thanks, Roxie. You'd better get going, or you'll miss your class."

She turned and sprinted out the door.

I turned to Jack and told him what I had just discovered about the carpet.

"What does it mean?" he asked.

"It's just a theory, but I suspect that someone came here and drugged Savanna, then carried her out to the loading area in the carpet. And I think it has something to do with this substance Savanna found. Someone didn't want Savanna or Roxie to know what they had, but I'm trying to figure out where Savanna got this mysterious substance, and what it was." I had two choices: either Savanna found the antidote, or she found the stash of zombie poison.

"So it was someone she knew," he said.

I shrugged and thought of Jonathan. "Probably."

I sat down at my desk and opened the file. Jack stood over me, reading over my shoulder and making the occasional comment. Just about every bit of information about my suspects was verified, with two exceptions: Francis Rathman had recently made a trip to Haiti—something his wife hadn't mentioned, or may not have known about—and Simon Lynch was not just a *hounsis*—he was a chasseur, or hunter. The chasseur brings the hunted in so that the decisions of the tribunal can be carried out.

Jean Toussaint was a poison maker and executioner. He never returned to Haiti. In fact, he disappeared altogether. I suspected he was here at

Hartmore. The question was, where? And was he still here of his own free will?

I thought about Jonathan and his antidote, his accusations about Kirsten stealing the antidote, and his thwarted plans to have Dr. Thompson test the antidote and discover the secrets that it held. I thought about Kirsten's accusations that the antidote wasn't any better than any other antidote she could get in Haiti. I dismissed Dr. Rathman as a suspect. He was a forensic anthropologist with a long career, and hadn't spent enough time in Haiti to become too involved in voodoo and *bizango*. He didn't have any apparent connection to Jean Toussaint, and only an indirect connection to Jonathan Sharpe, Kirsten Sorenson-Andersen, and Simon Lynch.

Then I thought of Dr. Cannon, who had brought me here to solve the mystery of the walking dead student, and the warnings my client began to receive shortly after that. And I thought about his own disappearance. And now Savanna had disappeared.

I turned to Jack. "Can you get a background on my roommate, Savanna?" I found a paper with her last name: Andersen. I sat down. I looked up at Jack and handed him the paper. He sat down beside me. "Do you think—?" we asked each other at the same time.

He nodded. I pointed to Savanna's computer. "Go ahead and use her computer. She's got a modem. I don't know how this fits into everything, but she's gotta be related to Kirsten Sorenson-Andersen. It's an unusual spelling for Andersen."

I looked at Savanna's schedule again and noticed that she had a class with Simon Lynch in a little over thirty minutes. While Jack got on the computer and went into the college registration files for Savanna's information, I checked Lynch's background sheet and discovered that he lived in on-campus housing, in a special loft built for visiting artists that was attached to the gallery.

"Jack, I need to go check something out. Will you be all right here?"

He got up and put his arms around me. "Where are you going?" He kissed the top of my head and looked worried.

"Please don't give me the mother hen routine," I said. I hate to be treated like a fragile piece of china.

He dropped his arms and looked hurt. "What?"

I sighed. "Sorry. I get a little weird when I feel smothered. You're gonna have to learn that about me if we keep seeing each other." What made me say that? We'd spent one night together. What made me think we'd have more than a passing few nights of comfort together?

He stepped back, looking hurt and angry. "Sorry to be concerned for your well-being."

I took his hand, and we sat down on the edge of my bed. "Jack, please be patient with me. I'm not used to someone, other than my mother, caring about me. I was in the marine corps and learned to take care of myself. For the most part."

He looked down. "It's just that," he paused and looked up, staring at the far wall, "well, I haven't felt this way about a girl in a long time." He looked sideways at me.

My mouth twisted into a smile; my stomach was doing flip-flops. "Yeah, I feel the same way."

We kissed, and it could have gone on that way for a long time, but I had a job to do, and Simon Lynch wouldn't be teaching that class forever.

FIFTEEN

WITH SOME DIFFICULTY, I left Jack and sprinted across campus to the gallery. It was quiet inside the gallery. There was no one around. I walked around the gallery, stopping at a collage here and a painting there. It was clear that Simon was a talented artist, but studying his art again, knowing he was a hunter for his society, made me see things in his work that I hadn't noticed before. I saw the figures in the background of his paintings—the lost souls, the walking dead, the zombies. I saw the snake in each picture—Damballah, the Father of Creation. I saw Erzulie, the Black Virgin, goddess of love, in several of the mixed media pictures. I saw Legba, the spirit of communication between the worlds, and Ghede, the spirit of the dead, and Ogoun Ferraile, the blacksmith god of fire and all things metallurgic.

I looked around the room and saw a door that I previously hadn't noticed. A shiver ran down my spine—all this mystical, menacing, weird stuff that

I had been involved with was finally getting to me. I took a deep breath and began to see things clearly. The door hadn't magically appeared—it had been here all along. I just was not looking for it during the party the other night, or it had been covered up by a painting or a flag.

When I walked over to it, I tried the handle. It opened easily. A stairway that led up to—could it be?—could this stairway lead to Simon's loft?

I looked around, but there was no one there. I called up the stairway, but no one answered. I closed the door and climbed the stairs. The soles of my boots sounded hollow against the wooden steps, echoes bouncing off the plain white walls. I stepped more carefully, trying to minimize the noise.

At the top of the stairs, the apartment opened up to me. There was no doorway, just a wide-open loft space with bare wooden floors and skylights to let in natural light. A standing screen cut off one corner of the room, where, I presumed, Simon's bed and personal possessions were kept.

The center of the apartment was completely bare with the exception of the altar, complete with candles, a *ve-ve* a sign drawn in cornmeal that represented the *loa* being called by the *houngan,* and several other voodoo-related pieces. Among these items was a bowl with a powder in it. I approached the altar and was about to reach for the bowl when a sound, a moan, made me freeze and turn around. Well, I started to turn around. But something large and heavy met my temple with great force, and I felt sick with the sound of the object echoing around the inside of my head. I put my hands out and fell to the wooden floor, then slowly fell into darkness.

SIXTEEN

I AWOKE TO the sound of chanting and drums. It was a tape or CD playing.

I tried to move my hands, but they wouldn't co-operate. Neither would my feet. I tugged at my bonds. It finally occurred to me that my hands were bound behind me and I was hog-tied, ankles to wrists. The room was dark. I must have been out for a couple of hours.

"Angela?" The voice was familiar. "Are you awake?"

"Yeah," I croaked. It came out more like "Unh." There was enough slack in the rope between my feet and my wrists for me to move a little bit. I was on my side, and I moved my knees up, then grabbed the bit of rope and pulled my torso back. I did this several times until I was facing Dr. Cannon.

He was tied up in the same manner as I was, lying on his side, and he didn't look very comfortable.

"Fancy meeting you here," I said, trying to put a brave face on the rising panic I felt. I had failed utterly at my job. And now I would become a zombie, sent to live in Haiti and pick sugarcane for the rest of my unnatural life.

"Angela, this is no time to joke." I noticed he had a bruise on his cheek and a split lip. "We have to get out of here."

I sighed and couldn't help saying, "Sorry, but I'm all tied up."

Dr. Cannon actually laughed. Then he got serious. "We have to get out of here, Angela. Haven't you noticed who else is here?" He turned his head, and I followed his gaze. My eyes had adjusted to the shadows, and I realized that it was almost dusk. Amy Garrett and a thin black man sat docilely in a corner. At least, I assumed it was Amy.

"Have you seen who's behind all of this?" I looked around and located my purse on a small table against the far wall.

"I'm guessing Simon Lynch, since we're in his loft."

"But he's only the chasseur."

"The hunter? My God, who is he hunting?" Dr. Cannon asked.

"Must be you. You're here."

"So are you," he pointed out.

"Is anyone else here right now?"

"No, they left."

"I was pretty sure you had stepped in the zombie powder by your bed," I said.

"This was a case of literally getting up on the wrong side of the bed," he said. "I normally get up on the side closest to the bathroom, of course. But the phone rang, and I'd left it in the living room."

"So you didn't walk through the powder," I concluded.

"No."

"Then how did you get here?"

"Savanna called and told me I needed to get down to her dorm room." Savanna must have been surprised when he answered the phone. But she had a backup plan. "She told me that Jonathan was ill—she described some of the symptoms of zombie poison. When I got there, I'm not sure about anything until I woke up here, hog-tied."

So Savanna wasn't the innocent she appeared to be.

"So did you know that Savanna is Kirsten's half sister?"

"Oh, yes," Cannon said.

"Why didn't you tell me?"

He probably would have shrugged if he could have. "I guess it didn't seem to be important. Look, the sooner you can figure out a way to get us out of here, the better. I get the feeling the ropes aren't a good thing.'' At least Dr. Cannon still had a sense of humor. But he seemed to think I was Superwoman.

I looked over at Amy, then turned back to Dr. Cannon. "Will she respond to directions?''

He nodded. "I think so, but nothing too complicated.''

I called her name softly. She was slow to respond, but she did finally look up. Her eyes were empty; her face was devoid of expression. "Amy, stand up and walk to the far wall until I tell you to stop.''

It took a moment, but she finally obeyed me. I watched as she shuffled across the floor, arms useless appendages at the ends of her shoulders, head down as if it were too heavy for her neck.

"Stop, Amy," I called out. She stopped where she was, just a few feet from my purse. "Now turn to your left and take two steps.'' She did as she was told until she was close to the table where my purse sat. "Pick up the purse in front of you.'' When she had the purse, I told her to bring it to me. She did. I wriggled around until I could open the purse up with my hands behind my back. I fished around inside until my hand closed around my pocketknife.

"Amy, put my purse back where you found it."

I didn't want Savanna or Simon walking in on me with my purse nearby.

"That's too broad an order," Cannon said as I twisted around so my back was to him. I scooted over until I was touching the ropes that held him. I opened the knife and began sawing away at my client's bonds as he ordered Amy to return my purse, then directed her to sit next to the other zombie.

"So who's the other guy?" he asked.

I was having trouble with the ropes—polyurethane proved difficult to cut with a blade. The rope gave too much, and the smooth blade had trouble grabbing the shiny surface.

"I think that's Jean Toussaint, the executioner who gave Jonathan the antidote."

"So he's the one who made the *contre poudre*."

I had finally sawed through one rope just about the time we heard footsteps on the stairs. I quickly scooted into a position facing away from the entrance, but kept my hands out of sight as I turned the knife blade around and twisted my wrists so the blade was hidden from sight unless someone looked closely at my bonds.

Savanna entered and looked down at me. She smiled.

"Hey, Savanna. And I was worried about you."

She giggled and spun around. "You didn't need

to be. I'm just fine.'' She leaned forward, and I wanted to rip her lungs out. ''But you need to be worried about yourself.''

Simon came into the picture. ''You've been a problem for us. Both you and Dr. Cannon here.''

''Why?'' I asked.

''Amy got out and wandered away a couple of times,'' Simon replied.

''Mostly because someone didn't give her enough of a dose of the zombie's cucumber to keep her docile,'' Savanna said in an accusatory tone. Then she smiled and let Simon wrap his arms around her waist.

''But everything worked out, didn't it?'' he said, nuzzling her neck.

''When does Kirsten appear?'' I asked, hoping a catfight over Simon would distract them.

''She doesn't,'' Savanna said airily. ''She's not a priestess. In Haiti, we had a local nanny who was a *premiere la reine,* first queen—quite high up in bizang. While she was busy with Nana's granny, picking plants in the hot sun, Nana was teaching me the basics of voodoo. I'm a *reine dirigeur.*''

''That's a directing queen to those who might not understand French,'' Dr. Cannon explained.

''Why are you doing this?''

Savanna extricated herself from Simon's grasp so that she could bend down to my level. ''Dr. Cannon saw Amy after her soul was stolen. I had already figured out that you weren't who you said you were.'' She shook her head and pouted. ''Besides, you are very nosy.''

''And Jean?''

She glanced at the pathetic figure in the corner. ''Our *bizango* society has declared that Jean must be punished. He not only gave away the antidote to Jonathan, he cast a *coup poudre* over Amy Garrett.'' She stood and addressed Simon. ''We need to do the ceremony.'' She strode across the room and disappeared behind the standing screen.

Simon crouched by the *ve-ve* to push the design back into order.

''Why are you doing this?'' I asked Simon. ''You have Jean Toussaint, why didn't you leave well enough alone?''

Simon shrugged. ''The *reine dirigeur* is the authority. She has ordered that we clean up the mess that Jean made.''

I was confused. ''What do you mean? Jean came here to get the antidote back and save face with his *houngan.* He did that.''

''Yes, but in doing so, this young woman, Amy, walked in on him, and he panicked. He gave her the zombie powder.''

This made no sense. Jean needed the *coup poudre,* but he didn't need to turn Amy into a zombie. If she walked in on his thievery, according to Dr. Cannon, it wouldn't have mattered because she didn't think the powder worked as an antidote anyway. It takes time and preparation to make a zombie, and I doubted that Jean kept a vial of zombie dust on hand for just such an occasion. If Amy walked in on him stealing the antidote, he might have hit her or beat it out of the house, but he wouldn't have automatically sprinkled her with zombie dust. And it would have given her time to tell Jonathan who had stolen the formula. Even Dr. Cannon had had warnings about keeping quiet about seeing Amy after she "died."

"Are you sure that Jean was the one who gave Amy the poison?"

Simon frowned. "Of course."

"You talked to him?"

"No," Simon said slowly. "The queen took care of him and told me after she'd stolen his soul. Why do you ask?"

"Savanna has shown an interest in Jonathan."

Simon shrugged. "The queen may have any man she desires."

"I don't think that Jean stole Amy's soul—I think your queen did. Savanna wanted Jonathan, and Amy was in her way." I shifted slightly. I'd been working on my bonds and almost had them cut through. I could tell that Dr. Cannon was working his ropes loose. "Tell me, did you get the antidote back?"

"My queen assures me that we did."

"Wouldn't surprise me if it was baking soda," I replied casually. "A girl could make a mint off of that formula, if it truly worked. And Jonathan is just the guy to string along to maneuver through the pharmaceutical jungle."

"No!" Simon replied, stopping what he was doing to look at me in anger. "She is a queen, and her loyalty is to her *bizango* society."

Savanna had returned, wearing a white shirt and blouse, the blouse tied up to bare her stomach. Her feet were bare, and her hair was loose. Yes, I now saw the resemblance to Kirsten. She strode toward us like a panther. It was now totally dark. I looked up briefly to see the stars beyond the skylights. Simon had lit all the candles, dozens of them all around the loft.

I had finally cut through my rope and was trying to get the feeling back in my hands and feet. I glanced over at Dr. Cannon, and he seemed to be trying to get the feeling back in his limbs as well.

I had the knife, though, and I was the Marine, so I had to make the first move.

Only I didn't have a chance.

"My Queen, I have heard lies about you, about your loyalty."

Savanna swayed her hips to the beat of the primitive music. "Is that so? And what rumors have you heard?" She turned around, dancing, writhing, young and sexy and powerful, a voodoo queen who had men falling at her feet. All but one. Jonathan.

"That you are the one who stole the woman's soul. That you have not returned the antidote."

She turned her back on Simon, bent down, then turned back and blew powder in Simon's face. He cried out, clutching his face, trying to wipe it off, clawing at his clothes. He staggered backwards, knocking over several candles in the process.

Meanwhile, I had subtly gotten myself into a position on my knees, my feet underneath me. Savanna didn't seem to notice, and Simon was way too busy to notice.

She was looking pretty proud of herself as she turned to me, a plastic glove covering her hand the poison had been carefully poured into; she held a vial of white powder in her free hand. She carefully poured another portion of it into her gloved palm. But she was busy looking at her hand, making sure she didn't stumble and get any of the poison on her. And she came close enough for me to take a deep breath and blow.

She screamed. The powder drifted toward her, but she quickly moved away before it drifted onto her skin. She didn't inhale it, but it was topical, and she looked at me in horror.

"You stupid bitch," she hissed.

She was breathing hard, panicking, but trying to keep some control. She stalked me, the vial of powder open, ready to throw at me. I rolled away from her and tossed the ropes. I stood up on wobbly legs. My feet tingled from getting the ropes off. I found it hard to walk without stretching first, but I didn't have a lot of time to work with.

Savanna came toward me, and I managed to keep away from her in the spacious loft, keeping the altar and the burning candles between us. She was so intent on getting her revenge on me for spoiling her plans that she seemed to have forgotten that Dr. Cannon and Simon were in the room. Cannon had finally gotten free of his bonds and was standing up.

Tears streaked Savanna's face. "You've ruined everything for me! I will cast a *coup l'aire* on you. Your hair will fall out, and your teeth will be crooked, and your children will all be deformed." I let her rant. She raised her vial to throw it at me, and I froze, ready to jump to the side. Simon staggered behind her, his hands still covering his face. Before she could hurl the zombie dust at me, Simon knocked into her, and the vial fell, spilling the poison on her skin. She fell toward the candles, and her skirt caught fire. The flame quickly ate at the cloth, and suddenly she was burning, spinning around out of control.

Somehow she managed to find Simon and grab onto him. "Help me! Help me! The fire!" Simon stood there and let the fire burn him.

I ran to the screen and looked for something to put the fire out. A quilt was draped on the futon bed. I grabbed it and ran back into the room, pushed the burning pair onto the floor, and threw the blanket over them. I threw myself over them and hugged the blanket, effectively putting out the fire. I could feel the heat, and the stench of loose bowels and urine emanated from the groaning, moaning pair. I rolled off of them and felt a stinging sensation in my arms. Looking down at them, I noted the burns and realized that aloe vera gel probably wouldn't take care of it. I felt a little sick and began taking deep breaths.

Dr. Cannon had found a phone, and I could hear him giving directions to the emergency operator. Then I passed out.

SEVENTEEN

I WOKE TO the smell of disinfectant and the sounds of people bustling by my door. I was in a hospital—Bristol General, I assumed, and my arms were bandaged.

Ma and Rosa were by my side. Ma was teary eyed, and Rosa was comforting her.

"Angela! Are you okay?"

I opened my mouth, and nothing came out. My throat felt raw.

"You inhaled some smoke," Rosa explained. She reached for a plastic glass and a pink plastic pitcher, poured some water, and stuck a straw in the glass before handing it to me.

I sipped it greedily, and my throat began to feel better. After a few minutes, I tried to talk again, this time slowly and in a whisper, "How long have I been here?"

"Since last night. It's two in the afternoon," Ma said. She blinked back more tears. "Angela, I want you to get out of this business."

I sipped more water. "Ma, before I left, you wanted to help me. Now you want me to go get a secretarial job."

She shook her head. "No, just a job with more security and less danger."

"Ma. This is not a normal case. Most of my cases are as dull as a pile of paperwork." I was getting agitated.

Rosa put her hand on Ma's arm. "Ma, why don't you go get us some coffee."

Ma gave Rosa a narrow look. "Since when did I become your maid?"

"Can't you see that Sarge is upset? She's just woken up." I was proud of my little sister—it was the first time I'd seen her stand up to Ma. And she was defending me.

"Ma," I said, "I love you, and I'll think about what you said. But would you please get me a coffee, black? I need to rest a few minutes, and Rosa can answer a few questions for me."

There was a hurt look in Ma's eyes when she finally left, and I felt like a complete dog for treating her like that. On the other hand, I was still healing, and she shouldn't have jumped on me when I was feeling vulnerable. I was actually questioning whether Ma was right about my choice of career, but it was something I would address later, when I had recovered.

"Sarge, don't listen to her. Ma's wrong."

I reached over and patted her hand awkwardly. "Thanks for the defense. But we need to talk about what's happened since."

Rosa nodded. "Your client has been sitting in the waiting room most of the time. The police have been here, asked him questions, and they want to talk to you when you feel up to it. And there's some cute guy who's waiting out there as well."

"What about the zombies?"

Rosa looked blank. "Maybe you'd better talk to Dr. Cannon before you talk to anyone else." She left to get him.

Ma came back with coffee for me. I thanked her profusely to make up for snapping at her earlier.

She gingerly kissed the top of my forehead. "I just worry for you. I get a call in the middle of the night, I'm told my daughter is in the emergency room of a hospital that's more than four hours away—what was I to think?"

"Thanks for coming, Ma."

She smoothed my hair back. "What was I supposed to do—allow you to lie in a strange place with no one to take care of you?"

"You're too good to me, Ma." The coffee felt good going down. The heat seemed to relieve the ache in my throat.

She sighed. "I know I shouldn't've told you how

to live your life. I know you can't change your career on the insistence of your mother.''

"Thanks, Ma."

"It's just when I heard what happened, even the silly part about zombies, I just couldn't believe you took this case."

"But didn't you see the zombies?"

She shook her head.

"Amy Garrett and Jean Toussaint?"

She gave me a strange look. "Are you feeling okay, Angela?"

"They should have been admitted here." I thought about it and realized that they had probably been flown to Boston—to Mass General or one of the other numerous hospitals that might have a specialist who could treat Amy and Jean.

Ma shook her head. "The only other people admitted were the two people who were badly burned."

"How are they?"

Ma shrugged. "How should I know?"

The door opened, and Dr. Cannon came in, followed by Rosa.

"You look better than last night," he said.

"So do you."

"I didn't quench the fire on those two."

"Yeah, well, I didn't want the place to burn down."

He chuckled. "Look, I talked to the president of Hartmore, and he said the college is taking care of your hospital bill."

"What happened to Amy and Jean?" I asked.

Cannon looked a little uncomfortable. "Can this be confidential?"

"I'm still working for you," I replied.

"After I called nine-one-one, I called Jonathan and told him to get down to the gallery as quickly as possible. I took Amy and Jean down into the gallery so they were out of the way when the paramedics arrived."

"So Jonathan has them?"

Dr. Cannon nodded. "Now we have to get the antidote back."

"The antidote wasn't in Simon's possession?"

"I was there when the police searched the place. Sergeant Zymm asked me to stay and help them identify the antidote. We did find what we think is zombie powder, and I'm having someone at the college test it."

"And Savanna didn't have it?"

He looked down. "We searched the room, but we didn't find anything. No powder, no list."

I lay back in my bed for a moment. The door opened, and Jack appeared with a bouquet of flowers. I smiled. He came over, and Rosa took the flowers from him and left to find a vase. Before she left, she turned around, and only I saw the thumbs-up she gave me. I suppressed a grin.

Jack leaned over me and kissed my lips. "You're looking better."

"If being awake means I look better, I'd better not fall asleep around you."

I forgot that Ma was there, and she stepped up. "Jack, this is my mother, Rosetta. Ma, Jack."

Ma sized him up, then looked over at me. "Is he interested in you or just a friend?"

"Ma!" Rosa came back. "Help me pick out a vase at the gift shop."

Ma eyed Jack. "Nice to meet you," she said before toddling off with Rosa.

I winced when she was gone. "Well, talk about being ambushed."

Both Jack and Dr. Cannon laughed.

I took a deep breath and said, "Well, this has been fun, but I need to get up and get dressed and get out of here."

"What are you talking about?" Cannon asked.

"We still have to find the antidote. Tell me, how're Savanna and Simon? Were they flown out of here to a Boston hospital?"

"They're both here until the doctors feel they're stable enough to be moved. Simon's doing all right. Some second-degree burns on his face and neck. But he's out of it, anyway," Dr. Cannon told me.

"The doctor almost pronounced him dead, but I got to the hospital in the nick of time to tell him about the tetrodotoxin poisoning."

"And Savanna?"

"She got the worst of it. Her hair is all gone, and she has third-degree burns," he said, taking off his glasses and shaking his head.

"Has she regained consciousness at all?"

"No. Kirsten is staying by her side, and her parents are flying up here from Haiti."

"Well, if you gentlemen wouldn't mind leaving for a few minutes, I'm going to get dressed." I slid out of bed, trying to be careful with my bandaged arms. I felt a wind at my back and realized that I didn't have a dressing gown. Fortunately, the men left me alone. My legs were shaky, but after a few moments of standing and walking, I got some of my energy back. By the time Rosa and Ma came back with the flowers in a vase, I had found my clothes and was partially dressed.

"Where do you think you're going?" Ma asked.

I felt like a rebellious teenager, caught red-handed with the keys to the car. Speaking of which, I had found my purse and was searching for said car keys. "I'm busting out of this joint," I replied.

Rosa giggled.

Ma was mortified. "Angela, the doctor said you needed more rest."

As if on cue, a woman in a white coat entered the room. "And how is the patient today?"

"Just fine, thank you," I said.

The doctor stopped and looked around. "Which one of you is the patient?"

I'd put on the long-sleeved sweater I'd originally been wearing, so it was hard to tell that I was hurt unless someone grabbed my arms.

Ma and Rosa both pointed to me. "She is," they said in unison.

The doctor approached me. She was a no-nonsense type with graying hair and glasses, sensible shoes, and a friendly smile. "You look like you're ready to leave here."

"You're not going to insist I stay, are you?"

She listened to my heart, shined a light in my eyes and in my ears, and stepped back. "Other than first-degree burns on your arms, you're in top shape. I'll just have to ask you to sign a form saying we're not responsible for your care after you leave us."

"Great."

"The papers will be at the front for you to sign when you're ready to leave." She smiled and left.

Ma and Rosa both had their arms crossed and didn't look happy with my decision.

"Look, I appreciate your coming up here," I told them, "but I have a job to finish. You can either go back to Boston or help me finish this investigation.''

They looked at each other, then back at me. ''We'll help out,'' Ma said.

I really didn't have anything they could do, but it was a way to keep them busy. I brought them out to Dr. Cannon and Jack.

''Ma and Rosa will stay with you, Dr. Cannon, while I work on finding the antidote for Jonathan.'' I raised my eyebrows for my client's benefit. ''I'm assuming that since the missing antidote is tied up with the case you originally asked me to investigate, you want me to pursue this?''

Dr. Cannon caught on quickly. ''Oh, yes. Of course. I'll just—have your mother and sister keep an eye on me.''

''Sort of like bodyguards,'' Ma said, pleased that she was contributing to my case. As they walked away, Ma was asking Cannon if he had ever tried stuffed artichokes. I had a feeling he would be eating very well tonight.

All that was left was Jack. He stood to the side, his hands in his pockets. ''That's your sister the art history major?''

''That's Rosa,'' I said.

''She's kind of cute,'' he said.

I jabbed him in the side. ''Don't go lookin' at my sister, bub. You got enough to handle with me." But as I said those words, I wondered what would become of our fast and fabulous relationship. Four hours away from Boston might as well be on the other side of the country.

Jack hugged me carefully. "So what's the next step?"

"The next step is for Angela to come down to the police station and talk to me." Sergeant Zymm had approached so quietly that Jack and I jumped.

"Hi, Pete," I greeted him. "Let's go now." I looked at Jack. "Maybe you should go over to Dr. Cannon's house, and I'll meet you there later."

He nodded, kissed my forehead, and warned Zymm, "Watch out for her forearms. She's been burned."

Zymm nodded and escorted me out the door.

I TALKED TO Zymm on the way back to the station. He asked questions; I answered to the best of my ability. I left Amy the zombie out of the story, though. And Jean the zombie. I'd had enough time to think about what Cannon had told me to make my story conform to his without sounding like a complete schizo.

"Okay, let me get this straight," Zymm said. "I know you were hired to look into the warnings that were being sent to Dr. Cannon. Along the way, you and Dr. Cannon figured out that it had something to do with a missing antidote for the poison that creates zombies, tetroda—'' He stopped there, unable to pronounce it.

''Tetrodotoxin.''

He shook his head. ''Right. That drug.'' He tapped his pen on the desktop. ''Is that it?''

I shrugged. ''I haven't found the antidote yet.''

''If you do, it would be worth a lot of money, wouldn't it?''

I shook my head. ''Not necessarily. It might not work. We only have Jonathan Sharpe's word for it. Is there anything else you need to know?''

Zymm looked down for a moment, then back up at me. ''I'll have your statement typed up by tomorrow. Don't leave town till you come back in and sign it.'' He stood up and shook my hand, then ordered a uniformed officer to drive me back to campus. I had the cop drop me off at my Bronco so I could get around on my own.

EIGHTEEN

I DROVE BACK TO the hospital. It was dinnertime, and the nurses were either checking patients who needed tests done or dispensing medication that needed to be taken with food. I had asked Dr. Cannon which hospital rooms Simon and Savanna occupied. Simon was right down the hall from me, and when I walked in, the room was empty with the exception of Simon in the bed.

"Simon?" I whispered.

He turned his head toward me. His face was bandaged, as were his arms and torso.

"Can you understand me?"

He nodded and grunted. Apparently the tetrodotoxin that hit him was wearing off. The skin that showed in between all the bandages was tinged with gray. As I got up close, I could see that his eyes had no light in them. I wondered how much he remembered, how much help he'd be to me.

"Simon, do you remember me?"

He hesitated, then nodded.

"Do you remember the antidote?"

Simon nodded more firmly.

"Do you know where it's hidden?"

He shook his head.

"What do you think you're doing?" An Oxford-educated accented voice asked me.

I turned around. "Hello, Kirsten. Just trying to get to the truth of where the antidote went."

She was wearing a pale blue blouse and a pair of black slacks. She crossed her arms, looking annoyed. "You won't get any information out of Simon. He's going to be in recovery for a long time."

I smiled. "Well, since he'll probably be transferred down to a hospital in Boston, I'll get more of a chance to visit him. I don't intend to let this go until I find out where that antidote is."

Kirsten scowled.

"And that goes double for your sister." I cocked my head and asked, "By the way, why do you have an accent and she doesn't?"

Kirsten's scowl faded, replaced by a slumping of the shoulders. "I went to college in England. Savanna has a gift for mimicking the local accent. Look, if I give the antidote to you, will you promise to leave both of them alone?"

I wondered if she knew that her beau, Simon, had a thing for her younger sister. I decided I wasn't going to tell her, because I hoped that by the time Savanna recovered, Simon would come to his senses and decide to stay with Kirsten.

I drove us back to Hartmore, to the social sciences building. Kirsten led me to her office and unlocked the door. It occurred to me that I hadn't brought my gun up to Vermont, on the thought that nothing I was going to investigate would be risky enough to warrant carrying a firearm. Now, as we climbed the stairs to the third floor and walked down the halls to her office, I was a little creeped out. I'd been tied up and almost turned into a zombie, and there wasn't anyone to whom I could ever tell that story who wouldn't laugh or call the funny farm.

Now, I thought about the fact that I hadn't told anyone I was going somewhere with Kirsten. But she didn't seem to notice. She was all business, unlocking her office door, turning on the light, and pulling out a file drawer. She handed me a package.

"So you did take it," I said.

She shook her head. "No. Savanna did. She hid it here, but neglected to tell me about it. I discovered it the other day, but I didn't know what to do with it."

I turned the envelope over in my hands, then opened it. A vial containing some gray powder was in the package.

"Thanks. Jonathan will be happy to have this back. He has several people who need the antidote." I looked up at Kirsten. Tears were streaming down her face. "Savanna took this from Jonathan. Did you know that she was a *bizango* queen?"

She nodded. "I suspected, but Savanna always loved secrets, and there has always been this competitive thing between us."

"That's why she didn't live with you?" I asked.

She shrugged. "That, and the fact that she was still an undergrad and it's college policy that students have to live on campus for their first three years."

"Did you know that your sister and Simon were involved in this whole mess?"

Kirsten shook her head. "I didn't know about Simon's role in all of this. I'm not sure what I feel for him now."

"When did you suspect Savanna had something to do with Amy's disappearance?"

Kirsten shrugged. "When you and I saw Amy across the street the other night, I suspected Simon more than Savanna. I knew my sister dabbled in the voodoo arts, but I didn't know she was a *bizango hounsis.* I guess Nana was teaching her about voodoo while I was gathering plants with Nana's grandma all those years."

We walked out. I was thinking that Kirsten

barely knew Simon—he'd only been here a few weeks.

"Well, you don't need to think about what to say to Savanna or Simon for a few weeks, maybe a few months. It'll take some time for them to recover."

"Maybe Jonathan will use some of the antidote on Simon, to speed his recovery." There was a hopeful note in Kirsten's voice. I doubted it, but I didn't say anything.

At least I didn't say anything encouraging about Jonathan and the antidote. But I had to say something to Kirsten. I stopped and faced her. "Kirsten, you can do better than Simon. I'm sure he's made you think you're lucky to have him, but trust me on this one: he's out for himself, and I doubt this experience will change his attitude. And your sister is a nutcase who thinks she's a *bizango* queen. Get her some help."

I turned and left.

I DROVE STRAIGHT to Jonathan and gave him the antidote. When he answered the door, he didn't let me in until I told him I knew he was nursing Amy and Jean Toussaint back to health. He looked like he hadn't gotten much sleep.

"They're doing better," he told me. "At least they're not being fed the zombie paste."

"Zombie paste?" I asked, not without a bit of

cynicism. I apparently hadn't read that far into the book.

"Zombie paste is fed to the victims to keep them under control," Jonathan explained. "The active ingredient is the zombie's cucumber, which has hallucinogenic properties."

I guess if I had been fed psychedelic pap, I'd be a zombie, too.

"So what are you going to do about Amy and Jean?"

Jonathan glanced behind him. "They should come out of it on their own, but I'm hoping the antidote will speed up the process."

"Will you be able to keep enough to test for its properties?"

He shrugged. "Getting Amy back, and helping Jean, are my first priorities."

"How will you explain Amy's being alive?"

Jonathan shook his head. "Maybe Dr. Cannon can help me with that. And Jean can't go back to Haiti. We'll have to contact some Haitian refugee society."

"Maybe Jean can remember the ingredients."

Jonathan shook his head. "It doesn't matter. Some pharmaceutical company would have just screwed it up anyway."

A shudder wriggled up my spine.

"What's the matter?" he asked.

"I came pretty close to being in Amy's shoes last night. So did Dr. Cannon."

Jonathan reached out and squeezed my shoulder. "Thanks for your help."

MY NEXT STOP was the room I shared with Savanna. I packed up and cleaned out my side of the room. Roxie stopped by.

"Hey, there's a rumor spreading around campus like wildfire—last night there was some kind of voodoo ceremony going on in the gallery when it went up in flames. Our resident artist and Savanna are in the hospital," she said, her eyes huge.

I smiled. "Yeah, something like that. Savanna will enjoy some notoriety, although I think she'll find it to be more of a liability than an asset in the long run."

Roxie seemed to think about it. She sat on Savanna's bed. "So what do you plan to do for the rest of your time here?"

"I still have a stop or two to make before I leave."

"That guy who was with you was frantic when you didn't come back. He called in the police, but they didn't believe him. He wasn't sure where you'd gone—" Yeah, I'd forgotten to tell Jack, but I hadn't planned to stay in Simon's loft long. Roxie trailed off, then added, "We both were going to form a search party when we heard the sirens."

I patted her shoulder. "Thanks, Roxie. Look me up if you come to Boston."

I left the dorm, my halcyon college days now over.

NINETEEN

THE MINUTE I walked into Dr. Cannon's house, I could tell Ma had been cooking. Cannon was seated with Rosa, and they were poring over a book of voodoo art. They looked up when I entered.

"Sarge! These voodoo flags are amazing pieces of primitive art," Rosa said.

Dr. Cannon raised his eyebrows mildly. "Sarge?"

"My nickname," I explained.

He stood up. "Thanks for everything. So it was Savanna who left the *wanga* for me?"

"Yeah. She must have gotten the key to your office from Amy after giving her the zombie poison. And after she retrieved Amy from the morgue—maybe there was a little remorse for what she'd done—Amy must have had enough sense to escape. Then Savanna had to chase down Amy and keep her out of sight until you were distracted. Getting the poison probably wasn't difficult—Simon must have brought some with him, just in case he needed it to subdue Jean Toussaint."

"And when you and Kirsten saw her?"

I shrugged. "I don't know. My guess is that Savanna was trying to move Amy from some other hiding place to Simon's loft. Maybe it had something to do with my moving in with her. When I arrived at the dorm, there were two beds that had been slept in. I don't know where Jean was in all of this, but I suspect that he'd been at Simon's loft all along. Savanna took one zombie; Simon had the other one. When I moved in with Savanna, she was very agitated that I was there."

"What were they planning to do with us once they had so many zombies?" Dr. Cannon asked. It was a rhetorical question, but I couldn't resist answering.

"There's plenty of jobs a zombie could do here in the States—any fast food restaurant, factory, or sweatshop would be happy to have us and would buy the paste to keep us silent and soulless for years to come." I shuddered again. "Let's just hope the government never decides to use tetrodotoxin for something like this."

He laughed.

Jack had been in the kitchen with Ma, helping her with the cooking and chatting about his plans for the future.

"I like him," Ma confided to me. "He's a young man with a future. You could do worse."

"Ma, if you endorse him any more, I may decide not to date him."

She patted the air. "Okay, okay. I'll keep quiet."

It was a feast. Ma can produce a repast out of bare cupboards that's worth talking about for years to come. I was starving and probably ate three times my weight in pasta and vegetables and veal.

When we were finished, Ma and Rosa told me they were driving back to Boston.

"You want to come with us, and we can come back up another weekend and pick up your car?" Rosa asked.

"Thanks, but I'm looking forward to driving back on my own. I'll be fine." We said a round of good-byes, Dr. Cannon promising Ma that he'd look her up when he came down to Boston next time.

After we saw them off, Dr. Cannon thanked me again.

Jack walked me out to the car.

"So, is this good-bye?"

I thought about it. "We don't live all that close. What do you think?"

He looked away briefly, then back at me. "I think I want to see you again."

"I don't have to leave right away," I said coyly.
"And there's this great bed-and-breakfast down the
road. We can discuss this relationship thing there."

He grinned and got in my Bronco.

LOOKING FOR

Chet Baker

AN EVAN HORNE MYSTERY
BILL MOODY

Pianist Evan Horne's European interlude lands him a gig in Amsterdam, where the old jazz clubs are alive and well. But here he unexpectedly finds himself reliving the last days of legendary blues trumpeter Chet Baker, who died under mysterious circumstances. Did Baker fall from a hotel balcony or was he pushed? The answers lead Horne on an odyssey into one of the greatest mysteries of the jazz world—and beyond.

"The book hits all the right notes...has the potential for turning mystery lovers into jazz fans."
—*Los Angeles Times*

Available March 2003 at your favorite retail outlet.

WORLDWIDE LIBRARY®

WBM450

Revenge
of the
Gypsy
Queen

A Tracy Eaton Mystery

KRIS NERI

The beleaguered daughter of eccentric Hollywood stars, mystery writer Tracy Eaton is no stranger to wacky people, especially within her family. So when her sister-in-law's wedding becomes a three-ring circus, Tracy is nonplussed, even when the bride is kidnapped.

Her snooty, bickering in-laws refuse to call the police and insist on paying the ransom. But Tracy knows that if justice is going to prevail, it will take all of her innate nosiness and nerve to get to the shocking truth—and the Eaton family secret.

Agatha, Anthony and Macavity Awards nominee for Best First Novel

Available February 2003 at your favorite retail outlet.

WORLDWIDE LIBRARY ®

WKN446

Love isn't always what it seems...

WITCHCRAFT

A VOLUME OF ELECTRIFYING MYSTERY AND ROMANCE
FEATURING A FULL-LENGTH NOVEL
BY *NEW YORK TIMES* BESTSELLING AUTHOR

JAYNE ANN KRENTZ

BONUS: two *original*, suspense-filled stories from

AMANDA STEVENS

REBECCA YORK

Look for WITCHCRAFT in March 2003.

HARLEQUIN®
Makes any time special®

Visit us at www.eHarlequin.com

PHW

Take 2 books and a surprise gift FREE!

SPECIAL LIMITED-TIME OFFER

Mail to: The Mystery Library™
3010 Walden Ave.
P.O. Box 1867
Buffalo, N.Y. 14240-1867

YES! Please send me **2 free books** from the Mystery Library™ and my free surprise gift. After receiving them, if I don't wish to receive anymore, I can return the shipping statement marked cancel. If I don't cancel, I will receive 3 brand-new novels every month, before they're available in stores! Bill me at the bargain price of $4.99 per book plus 25¢ shipping and handlng and applicable sales tax, if any*. That's the complete price and a savings of over 10% off the cover price—what a great deal! There is no minimum number of books I must purchase. I can always return a shipment at your expense and cancel my subscription. Even if I never buy another book from the Mystery Library™, **the 2 free books and surprise gift are mine to keep forever.**

415 WDN DNUZ

Name   (PLEASE PRINT)

Address   Apt. No.

City   State   Zip

* Terms and prices subject to change without notice. N.Y. residents add
  applicable sales tax. This offer is limited to one order per household and not
  valid to present Mystery Library™ subscribers. All orders subject to approval.
© 1990 Worldwide Library.
™ is a trademark of Harlequin Enterprises Limited

MYS02

Bestselling Harlequin Presents® author

LYNNE GRAHAM

Brings you one of her famously
sexy Latin heroes in

DARK ANGEL

This longer-length story is part of
the author's exciting *Sister Brides*
miniseries! Convinced the
Linwood family framed him for
embezzlement, business tycoon
Luciano de Valenza seeks
revenge against them. His plan:
to take everything that is theirs—
including their daughter, Kerry!

*Look for DARK ANGEL
in March 2003!*

HARLEQUIN®
Makes any time special®

Visit us at www.eHarlequin.com   PHDA

A RANSOM/CHARTERS MYSTERY

THE MUMMY'S RANSOM

FRED HUNTER

In a philanthropic push to sidestep his negative image as a destroyer of Chicago's famous landmarks, real estate mogul and Chilean expatriate Louie Dolores brings an exhibit of ancient Chinchorro mummies to his huge downtown skyscraper. But when a "mummy" comes to life and starts haunting the exhibit, Chicago detective Jeremy Ransom uses his street smarts—plus the keen insight of his trusted confidante, the elderly Emily Charters—to start questioning those who might want to cause trouble.

"Series fans will be well pleased..."
—*Publishers Weekly*

Available March 2003 at your favorite retail outlet.

WFH451